Oranges from Spain

DAVID PARK

JONATHAN CAPE
LONDON

for Alberta

First published 1990
This paperback edition first published 1991
Copyright © David Park 1990
David Park has asserted his right
to be identified as the author
of this work
Jonathan Cape Ltd, 20 Vauxhall Bridge Road, London SW1V 2SA

A CIP catalogue record for this book
is available from the British Library

ISBN 0–224–02765–4 (Hardback)
ISBN 0–224–03156–2 (Paperback)

Phototypeset by Computape (Pickering) Ltd, North Yorkshire
Printed in Great Britain by
Mackays of Chatham PLC, Chatham, Kent

Oranges from Spain

Fair seed-time had my soul, and I grew up
Fostered alike by beauty and by fear.

Wordsworth, *The Prelude*

CONTENTS

THE TRAP

His FATHER sat with his legs stretched out into the hearth, his stockinged feet so close to the crackling furnace of a fire that steam rose in steady wisps. He was still wearing his working clothes, and the bottoms of his corduroy trousers were ringed with mud which would eventually harden and flake off about the house. He sat in his armchair at the side of the chimney where only a stranger, ignorant of its private ownership, would dare to sit. As he watched his father dozing, his head jerking at intervals on to his chest, he noticed how soiled and threadbare the headrest had become, worn almost shiny with use, and the white circles on its wooden arms where for twenty years his father had rested his mug. While all the meals were taken at the white-clothed table, his father always moved to the armchair for his tea. It did not matter whether there was company or not, he never broke his habit, and while select visitors might take their tea out of the best rose-patterned teaset, he would insist on his bucket of a mug.

'Sure, those dainty wee cups are no use to a man at all. A couple of mouthfuls and you're looking at its bottom,' he would say, with a dismissive wave of his hand.

As he dozed now, his head lolling to one side, the fire lit up the weathered tautness of his face and the tracery of tiredness circling his eyes, and even in this fitful drowse, it was as if his body was struggling to fight off some deeper sleep.

In the kitchen he could hear his mother setting the washed dishes back in the cupboard and the tinkle of cutlery dropping into the drawer. When she had finished she too would come and sit by the fire. A little section of it caved in on itself, and his father's breathing grew heavier. In a short while, however, he

1

would wake up and say something like, 'Boys-a-dear, I'm fair bushed the day,' and then shuffle off to find some work to do, as if feeling guilty about the time he had wasted. He was a man whose whole life was founded on work; without it he was a floundering confusion. Take it away from him and he was like a little boy lost in a foreign and unfriendly city, where nothing was familiar and nothing had purpose. Away from the farm he wallowed in misery. There was, too, a deep vein of arrogance in him which produced an unshakable conviction that no one was able to do things as well as he could. Certainly not his son. He had also, just below the surface, a temper which could blow sudden and fierce, and which as a child he had often experienced, usually for the crime of 'answering back'. His father grunted in his sleep and his mouth opened slightly.

He got up and drew back a curtain from the window, but it was dark outside and all he saw was his own reflection. Carefully, he pulled it closed again, making sure it overlapped with the other one, not leaving a gap, which would irritate his mother. She was a patient, quiet woman who rarely complained about anything – perhaps she felt as if the outside world would be able to see into the room through any chink and observe them secretly. The thought gave him a little shiver and he ran his hand down the curtains' join, making sure the folds fitted neatly over each other. He sat again and stared into the fire. Great glowing caverns of red were opening up under the thinning layer of slack. A puff of soot fell into it. The clock chimed. His mother came in with her sewing box under her arm and sat down. Without speaking, she handed him the needle to thread and then began to mend a ripped knee in a pair of blue overalls.

'Did you put in much new fencing today?' she asked, without looking up from her work.

'Aye, a good bit – mostly up round the top fields. I'm sorry about the overalls. I never work with the wire but I tear something on it.'

She smiled and smoothed the overalls with her hand.

'At least you didn't cut your hands. It's terrible stuff to work with, all right.'

2

He looked at her with some surprise.

'Have you worked with it, then?'

'I was working with it before you were born. Who do you think helped your father fence along the front road?'

In his imagination he struggled to picture this slight woman grappling with fence poles and wire, but he could not focus on a clear image. She looked up and caught the quizzical look on his face.

'We couldn't afford any outside help in those days. Anything that had to be done we did ourselves. At harvest time your Uncle Tommy would lend a hand but that was all.'

His father grunted again. They both glanced at him, then smiled at each other, momentarily linked in a little conspiracy of friendship which excluded the sleeping man. She returned to her sewing, forming close, delicate stitches which cut no corners or hurried anywhere. Doing a job well was a matter of honour – in that, his parents were well-matched. The slipshod, the lazy – all were despised as sins against God.

'A job done half-right is a job done half-wrong,' she would say to him when he was a child, applying her measuring rule to some task he had botched or executed half-heartedly. He hadn't heard her say those words for some time. He watched her as she sat with her head bent over the sewing. It unsettled him to see how old she was beginning to look. It had hit him first on his return from his second year at university. Like most sons who loved their mother, he had assumed that she would go on for ever, unchanging and untouched by time or illness. It was only when he had returned and looked at her with fresh eyes that he realised he had been carrying an image of his mother which was unaltered since childhood. It was an image of someone strong, both inside and out; the woman who for twenty years was the first to rise, who lit the fire and had breakfast cooking on the stove each morning; the woman who was never ill and who never seemed to have any desires or needs beyond providing for the welfare of her family. It was the warm comforting memory of the mother who nursed him when he was ill, and salved the wounds his father's sharp-edged tongue had inflicted. As he looked at her now, he

3

saw a woman whose hair was whitening like a frosted hedgerow, and whose hand shook when she tried to thread a needle. There was still an inner wick of strength, but it no longer burned so brightly or seemed so invincible.

More of the fire caved in. Soon, it would be time to build it up again. He hoped the coal scuttle didn't need filling, or it would mean a trip out to the wintry yard. His father started to wake up, and rubbed his mouth with the back of his hand. The chair creaked as he pushed his back into it. His mother paused from her sewing. Suddenly, the dog started to bark loudly in the kitchen, then followed a high-pitched, nervous whine. His father jumped up and grabbed his boots, and without opening them, forced his feet down into them, stamping on the floor to get them on, as if crushing some poisonous insect.

'He's here! Samuel, get the gun, quick. Quiet, boy, quiet!'

The dog stopped barking, but continued to let out a faint, tremulous whimper. As his father rushed into the kitchen, he fumbled with the catch of the gun cupboard, trying to open what was firmly locked. His mother threw down her sewing and got the key from its hiding place inside the fruit bowl. With it, he opened the door and pulled out his father's shotgun. As he hurried out with it, his mother called him back.

'The cartridges, Samuel, the cartridges!'

He ran back and grabbed the box, almost dropping it in his haste. His father was standing in the kitchen with the light out, peering into the yard. The dog stood alert and ready, but completely silent. He loaded two cartridges and handed the gun over. His father checked it with a glance, then ordered the dog to stay. Opening the door only wide enough to allow both of them to edge through, they slipped into the yard. The cold night air stung their faces and a cutting wind stabbed at their clothes. A bright, whole moon cast a milky light over the yard and sharp-iced stars trembled nervously. They walked slowly towards the barn, their eyes scanning every shadow for any flicker of movement, and their ears straining for the slightest rustle, but a silent stillness held everywhere, calm and undisturbed. His father carried the shotgun loaded and ready to fire, holding it out in front of him but pointed at the ground. His breathing was heavy and there was a stiffness in his stealthy movements which made them seem awkward and exaggerated. As a cloud scudded across the moon, they paused and stared into the pools of darkness which formed at the base of the barn and round the sheds and outhouses beyond it. Glancing at each other, they shook their heads to say they saw nothing, then his father nodded in the direction of the hen-run. Suddenly, there was movement close to the furthest shed, and the shotgun sprang up into the shooting position.

'It's only one of the cats, Da,' he cautioned.

But it was too late, the barrel had already spurted red, and with a loud crack sent a volley of shot that splintered the stillness which had settled on the surface of the night. The cat scuttled off unharmed into deeper darkness.

'Damnation!' spat his father, the closest he ever came to a public curse. 'Thon cats are a damned nuisance – always getting in the road of something. They're not worth their keep. If it'd got itself killed, it would've been good value for it.'

They walked openly and quickly, both knowing that if the fox had been there, it was now long gone. They checked the hen-run and looked around but could find no trace of an attempted incursion.

'Come on – there's no point freezing to death out here. It'll not come back the night, but we'll let the dog out to run round for a hour or so just to be sure.'

'Are you certain it was here?'

His father looked at him as if he had just asked a foolish question.

'It was here, all right. The dog knew and as soon as I set foot in the yard I knew too. It was here all right – as sure as I'm talking to you now.'

They turned back to the farmhouse, walking in silence and occasionally passing a little shiver from one to the other. When they got into the living room, the fire had been built up and the hearth brushed. His father returned to his armchair but sat on its edge and held his open palms towards the heat.

'He's a fly one, all right – I'll give him that. But I'll get him in the end. Sooner or later, he'll make a mistake, then I'll burn his tail.'

'The radio forecast snow,' his mother said. 'If it does, it'll make finding food harder than it is already. When he's desperate he'll be driven down here and ready to take risks.'

His father nodded in agreement, then leaned forward and spat into the fire. It sizzled for a second then vanished. Silence settled on the room. His mother finished sewing the overalls and began to darn the thick woollen socks his father always wore, summer or winter. His father began to study seed catalogues, pausing from time to time to complain about price increases from the previous year. While his parents did this, he sat at the table and began to read some of his lecture notes. Finals were only six months away, and he was already a little nervous. Although he pretended not to see it, he caught his father winking at his mother, as he always did when he saw his son studying, as if somehow he was engaged in a slightly humorous activity. Once, he had caught his father flicking through one of his textbooks and, when he realised he had been discovered, he dropped it red-faced, saying, 'A powerful lot of words, a powerful lot. And is anybody the wiser for them?' Despite his father's outward indifference, he suspected that he harboured some well-hidden pride in it. Once, at market, he had overheard him giving William McBurney a list of the subjects he was studying, pronouncing each one slowly as if it was a foreign word he had to get exactly right.

The silence thickened and deepened in the room. He looked up from his notes and thought about the fox. He wondered where it was at that exact moment – perhaps slinking through some sheltering hedgerow, or looking down at the yellow-eyed farmhouse from the dark safety of the woods. He had seen it only once. It was during the summer, when, sitting on the back of the baler, he had glanced down to the bottom meadow, and to his amazement had spotted the fox trotting across the field, pausing only to sniff a little circle of itself. Even allowing for the distance, it was smaller than he had imagined, but there was something almost arrogant about its strut through the sharp-spiked stubble.

But he harboured no romantic fancies about it and would kill it too if he got the chance. It was vermin and had to be destroyed. Anyone who had seen the hen-coop that morning couldn't help but feel the same way. Last August, the fox had broken in and butchered a dozen hens, killing with a savagery that was fired by a need beyond hunger. When he discovered it, it had been all he could do to stop himself being sick. For his father, this was the beginning of something which started as a desire to protect his property and livelihood, but gradually turned into an intensely personal battle where wits were pitted against each other, until it became almost a struggle for supremacy over the land itself. There were mornings when his father rose at dawn and stalked the hillsides, hoping for some chance sighting. He would stand in the shadows, for an hour or more, close to any spot where he had found some trace of it, his patient determination stronger than any discomfort.

When his father finished studying the seed catalogues, he raised himself slightly off the chair, slipped them under the cushion he was sitting on, and in the same movement brought out a copy of the local newspaper. He got a full week out of it, confining his nightly reading to a separate section. This evening, he read the council news and scrutinised the planning applications, commenting from time to time to no one in particular, on their relative merits.

'Jim McCammon has put in again for a bungalow on the Ballymore Road.'

'They'll never let him build there,' replied his mother.

'I don't know about that. He was telling me last week he's got Hugh Downey pulling for him in the council, and somebody in the planning office told him he'd a fair chance.'

'Wheels within wheels,' said his mother, enigmatically.

'Aye, it's all about who you know these days,' his father asserted. Then, lifting the poker from the side of the hearth, he raked it backwards and forwards between the lowest bars of the grate. 'I was thinking of putting in myself,' he said quietly, sitting back casually, but alert to register what reaction his words had evoked. Looking up from his lecture notes, he saw that his mother had stopped darning and had a look of surprise on her face.

'For a building site?' she asked.

'Aye, a building site for a house or a bungalow.'

'And where would the site be?'

'Well now, I've always thought down by Miller's Lane would be a quare good site for a house. You've a brave view and you're close to water and electricity. It's a quiet road, but it's not as if you're out of the way or anything.'

No one spoke.

'I'm only thinking about it, now. I haven't decided on anything yet. But you never know when a site could come in useful.'

His mother returned to her darning with a thoughtful concentration and his father turned another page of the paper. The fire glowed deeply red and the only sound which broke the silence was the chime of the clock.

The radio forecast was right. In the morning there was a light skim of snow brushing the ground and icicles hanging from the guttering of the house. In her habitual response to snow, his mother had made porridge for breakfast, and they took it with warm milk and a lacing of sugar, while steaming logs crackled and hissed in the fire. He had offered his father a morning's work – he needed the rest of the day to work on an essay due at the start of the new term. As he finished his last piece of toast, his father was lacing his boots and warming his palms at the fire, then rubbing them together as if to store up heat for the rest of the day.

'Well, let's get at it, then. If you're on a half-day, I'd better get the most out of you.'

'Studying's hard work too,' he said defensively.

'What was it old Dan McCoubrey used to say about scholars?'

He pretended to search in his memory before answering his own question, a smile fingering the sides of his mouth.

'"The pen's lighter than the spade, for learning's easy carried" – aye, that was it. I mind it now.'

He put on his overcoat, placed his flat cap squarely on his head, then pulled it down until the peak shadowed his eyes.

'Aye, those were his very words. I mind it well, now,' he said, as he opened the kitchen door and strode off across the yard, his sturdy footprints crisply cemented in his wake.

His good mood did not last long. The tractor engine refused to start, its blackened innards groaning and whirring at each attempt to force it into life. It had given good service over many years, but it was obvious it would not survive the strain of many more winters. Finally, however, it stuttered into half-hearted life and they loaded bales of hay on to the trailer and set off down the long lane to the fields. As always, snow seemed to make the world quieter, stiller, a unified one-ness through which their noisy journey seemed clumsy and intrusive. The passage of the tractor between the hedgerows dislodged little flurries of snow and, long after they had passed, the snow continued to fall like a fading echo. In a white-humped field, two rabbits traced intricate patterns, then scampered over the brow of the hill, kicking up tiny spumes of snow as they ran. The sky was full of the promise of more snow.

The tractor trundled on to the lower fields. The cold air burnt their faces and they were glad when they had strewn the last of the fodder across the frozen ground. His father's breathing was loud, and he laboured over the final few bales, his breath streaming in front of him. Two grey-backed crows watched them from the naked branches of an ash tree. His father caught them in the corner of his eye but looked away again, then walked casually to the trailer where he had stored the shotgun. Keeping the tractor between himself and the tree, he loaded the gun, his cold fingers fumbling with the cartridges, then stepped out into the open. But before he could shoulder it, the two crows had wheeled away, slicing the air as their mocking squawks broke the surface of the silence like stones dropped in water.

'They've an eye in their head like a hawk,' he mumbled to himself, feeling slightly foolish. 'The worst creatures God ever made. If they're not stripping the barley, they're pecking the eyes out of newborn lambs.'

'They're ugly things, all right,' he agreed. 'But they're too sharp to shoot out in the open at this distance.'

His father grunted non-committally and unloaded the gun.

They continued on and did a check of all the stock, stopping to fix a broken gate by tying it up temporarily with wire. A weak, hazy sun was trying to emerge but it failed to bring any warmth to the morning. They didn't talk much and the clatter of the tractor engine gave them an excuse for silence. As they headed back towards the farm a single swan lolloped overhead. He pointed it out to his father, but he acknowledged it only with a disinterested nod of his head.

When the tractor was making its way up the narrow lane to the farmyard, his father stopped suddenly and got down from the tractor. He bent over like a man searching for a lost coin, and moved along the verge, touching the snow occasionally with his hand.

'It's been here. Look!'

'Are you sure? Could it not just be a dog?'

'I know the marks of a fox when I see it,' his father snapped, his voice barbed with irritation. 'And it'll be back up round those hens before too long. Mark my words!'

They put the tractor back into the shed and covered the engine with old sacking. In the house, his mother served up deep plates of freshly made vegetable soup, thick with barley and carrots, and the tops of potatoes sticking up like icebergs. She wore a pair of woollen socks over her tights and a pair of fur-lined ankle boots with a zip up the front. His father talked constantly of the fox.

After lunch, his father went into the yard to chop logs, and he offered to help him for an hour. They set up two chopping blocks and started into the pile. He could not help but admire the repetitive, mechanical accuracy with which his father quartered the logs, and knew his own efforts fell short of that standard. But he did his share and slowly the pile of uncut logs dwindled to nothing. They carried out the trunk of a tree they had felled the previous summer, and using a cross-cut saw, began to divide it into workable sections. He could feel his father's strength as his shoulder pushed the saw towards him through the wood and he tried to match it as he pushed it back. The blade cut straight and deep, and as snow began to fall lightly, the push and pull bedded itself into a steady rhythm. Tiny chips of wood sprayed on to the snow. Backwards and forwards it cut, the blade never jumping or jerking. Then gradually, almost imperceptibly, he sensed that his father's push towards him was weakening. He glanced up at his face and saw it tight and pained. Flakes of snow had whitened his hair. He looked suddenly old. His father was holding on grimly to the saw, determined to see the job finished. As his father pushed the saw once more towards him, he held it tightly and did not push it back. His father pulled, then looked up at him with confused, watery eyes. Neither of them spoke. His father pulled again, but he held the saw fast and did not let it move.

'We've cut enough logs for one day, Da. We'll go inside now,' he said, his voice stronger and surer than he really felt.

His father said nothing, but straightened himself up and brushed snow off the front of his coat as if it was a stain. He seemed unsteady and uncertain of what direction to take. Leaving the saw embedded in the wood, he took his father by the arm, and, shoulder to shoulder, they walked slowly towards the house. His mother seemed to know what had happened before he had time to tell her. They helped him into his chair and she knelt at his feet and gently removed his boots.

'No need for fussing, now. It's just a wee tightness. In a few minutes I'll be as right as rain,' his father reassured her.

'You're stopping there the rest of the day,' ordered his mother in a voice which brooked no argument.

She poked the fire to let air in underneath and then brushed flakes of snow off him with a towel from the pile of ironing she had stacked in the corner of the room.

'I'm all right now, Cassie, no fussing,' he said, looking with embarrassment towards his son. 'I'll just take one of those wee sweeties the doctor gave me and in a few minutes I'll be up and running.'

He watched his mother scuttle into the kitchen and return with the tablet and a glass of water. His father swallowed the tablet, throwing his head back, and his mother held the glass to his mouth while he drank.

He went back out to the yard, cleaned the saw and stacked the logs, filling a bucket for the house. When he returned his father was sleeping, watched over by his mother as she did the ironing.

'How long's this been going on?' he asked, conscious that things had been kept from him.

'He first got a pain about a year ago – well, that's when I found out about it. Dear knows how long he had it before then, and a right furore there was before I got him to go to the doctor's. It's his heart, but everything could be all right if he's sensible and doesn't overdo things.'

'But why did you not tell me?'

She stretched a shirt over the ironing board.

'We decided there wasn't any point worrying you with something you couldn't do anything about. And you've enough on your mind with your studies.'

'But I could've come home more weekends than I did, and helped out more.'

'It's not the weekends he needs help – it's the five days in between.'

She readjusted the shirt almost angrily.

'What about Ivan? Isn't he supposed to help about the place?'

She spat on the iron.

'Your father let him go. He was no use, Samuel. There wasn't any work in him, and if he'd been out gallivanting the night before, he wouldn't turn up before lunchtime. He brought your father more aggravation than help.'

'You're going to have to get some decent permanent help. Things can't go on like this.'

'Easier said than done. Anybody able round here's got their own place to look after, and your father's not an easy man to work with. I don't have to tell you that. He likes things done his way – always has and always will.'

They both glanced at the sleeping man. His passive tranquillity seemed at odds with the words she had just used. She continued ironing and as she smoothed invisible creases and wrinkles he knew that she was working up to saying something – something important. She hesitated, then set the iron on its heel, rubbing her hand along the ironing board.

'Your father – well, both of us – have always hoped that after you got your education you'd come back and run the farm with him. In a few years, maybe, take it over. He's a proud man, and he'll never ask, but it's what he's always wanted. I suppose that's what that site business was all about. One thing's for sure – if he goes on like he is now, he'll kill himself.'

There were tears in her eyes, and she tried to hide them by snatching a towel out of the basket and shooting the iron up and down it.

'I've never asked you for anything before, Samuel, but I'm asking you now. Asking you just to think about it – even for a year or so, until we get something sorted out.'

'My heart's never been in farming, Ma – you know that. I've never wanted to make it the rest of my life. I've always done my share, but . . . it's not even as if we get on well together.'

'Your father's not a man who shows his feelings, and I know he hasn't always been easy on you, but I know, deep down, he's proud of you. When you got to university there wasn't a body on the road he didn't tell.'

'He'd never be able to sit back and hand the running of the farm over to me. You know he'd – '

His mother motioned him to be quiet. His father was stirring in the chair and rubbing his mouth with the back of his hand, as if to get rid of some bad taste.

'All I'm asking you to do is think about it. That's all,' she said softly, as she folded the towel and set it neatly on the top of the finished pile.

'Boys-a-dear, I must've dropped off,' his father said, stretching out his legs, as if nothing had happened. 'It's the heat of that fire brings it on. Is it still snowing outside?'

'It is, and you'll not be stirring over the door,' asserted his mother with an intense quiver of feeling.

'Will you stop fussing, woman. I'm right as rain.'

But for the rest of the afternoon, he pottered aimlessly about the house, listening to the radio and occasionally stopping to stare out of the window. After tea, his talk turned again to the fox.

'Thon same boy'll be back the night. I feel it. He's got the scent of those hens and he won't give up until he's got a couple for his supper. I think we'll have a wee surprise waiting for him.'

'You're not planning to be running about on a night like this, when anyone with the ounce of sense they were born with'll be sitting by their firesides?' his mother complained.

'Hush, now, there'll be no running around. I'm going to set the trap.'

His father must have caught the look on both their faces, because he tried to reassure them.

'There's no need for worry. I'll be careful with it. The dog'll be locked up and if it'll keep everybody happy, we'll shut all the cats in the barn until the morning.'

His father had used the illegal gin trap, a relic of days long gone, with a marked lack of success. Its rusty but lethal teeth had a tendency to snap shut on creatures other than those for which they were intended. Magpies, in particular, greedy for the bait, had a habit of losing a wing or even their heads in its undiscriminating jaws. Yet his father believed that it could be relied on in a time of crisis to tip the balance in his favour. When all his best efforts had failed, he turned to it with a persistent faith, ignoring its record of failure.

Later that evening, the trap was brought down from the high shelf of the barn, where it sat with the plastic container of paraquat, and the dust was blown off it. His father handled the trap with respect and, to check it was still working, set it on the barn floor, then poked a thin stick warily on to the release plate. The predatory teeth sprang shut with a shuddering clack, snapping it cleanly in two, and leaving a ringing silence in its train. He carried the trap out into the snow-blanched night, and after making sure dog and cats were safely locked up, set it close to the hen-run, baiting it with the remains of the chicken which had made lunchtime soup. He chained the trap to an old wheelbarrow, kicking snow over as many parts of it as he could. Watching his father at work pushed a sudden shiver through him, and he was glad when the job was finished. His father made no reference to the earlier events of the day, and now he slipped into that bantering tone which he liked to employ.

'I take it you'll not be going for any moonlit walks?'

'No, I wouldn't think so.'

'Aye, it'd be a bad night for sleepwalking. Wouldn't want you hopping round the halls of learning with one foot.'

They walked back quickly to the house, their footsteps crunching the freezing snow. Then, as the evening began to take its normal course, he told his parents he was going to have an early evening. It was true the extra work he had done for his father had left him tired, but he also needed an escape from the somnolent, stifling atmosphere of the room, to where he could work and think clearly.

He tried to study, but his mind was unable to concentrate for more than a few minutes, always returning to what his mother had said. He had never seen her cry before and it hurt him to think of it. Her tears fell in his memory like slow flakes of snow and piled up in deep drifts about his heart. All his own conviction faded away as they fell across his intended road, blanking and whitening out the landmarks he had set in his future, and leaving him unsure and confused about what direction to take. When, eventually, he fell asleep, his restless dreams were a web of fragmentary images in which he found himself lost in a tangle of tall hedgerows, whose thorns reached out to scratch his arms. As he struggled to escape he could feel the burning yellow eyes of the fox following and watching him through the chinks of the hedge. In his dream, he knew that somewhere sitting waiting was the cruel trap, its perfect teeth glinting in the moonlight. While he dreamed, snow continued to fall. It dropped steadily, filling up the laneways and silently layering the roof above his head.

In the morning his father rustled with impatience to inspect the trap. He blew on each spoonful of porridge to cool it, and then slurped it noisily. A tiny dribble of milk ran down his chin and he wiped it away with the back of his hand. The radio spoke of roads being closed and isolated communities cut off. Going to his armchair, his father warmed his stockinged feet, then struggled into the boots which he had cleaned the night before. He laced them carefully, jerking the laces tightly at each set of eyelets, then pulled up his heavy socks as far as they would stretch. He seemed anxious that his son should come with him, so, as his father stood fidgeting over him, he finished his tea and put on his coat. Snow had drifted against the kitchen door and when they opened it some fell across the mat. The familiar world they instinctively expected had vanished, to be replaced by a foreign world which swaddled their senses and dazzled their eyes. As he followed his father round the sheds to the hen-run, he felt suddenly frightened by what they might find.

The trap was closed – he could see it in the distance. He felt an inexplicable surge of relief. There was no fox in it. But, as they drew closer, they saw dark splashes of blood spotting the snow. His father ran, and kneeling over the trap, cleared away the snow with his hands, like a child digging in sand. Then he swore in a deep, fierce way, spitting the words out like they were bitter to his tongue, as with frightened eyes, he stood aside to show him the fox's paw his hands had uncovered.

'God in heaven, he's eaten through his own paw to escape. He's gnawed his own paw right off. I've heard of it, but I'd never have believed it, only I'm looking at it with my own eyes,' his father said, his voice quiet but his hands shaking. 'Go and get the gun and the dog. We'll follow the trail back up to its den. We've got him now.'

Then he turned and knelt once more over the trap.

'I'll get no gun. I'll take no part in this,' he said, his voice cutting high and clear through the cold air. 'I'll have no hand in its killing.'

His father stood up, his eyes red and raw, his fists clenched by his sides as if he was going to strike him. Words started to his lips but melted away into nothingness. Suddenly, he turned and, without speaking, headed back the way he had come. For a second he watched his father's heavy trudge across the snow as black shadows of crows circled overhead, and birch trees shivered on the skyline. He looked at the trap again. Then he turned and followed his father, leaving his own prints in the snow.

KILLING A BRIT

'KIERNAN CAFFREY, this homework is a slovenly insult to your Maker. Stay in this afternoon and do it properly.'

Kiernan Caffrey did not lift his head but continued to stare blankly at his open jotter, determined not to let Father Brophy see his disappointment. He had known, however, that it was only a question of time before he received this sentence. He had managed to slip his homework into the bottom of the pile, but when they returned from lunch Father Brophy had set them a composition and settled himself comfortably behind his desk to mark them. From the start, he had known that his homework would not be acceptable, but he had scrawled a half-hearted attempt at the questions, only in order to avoid the cane. Now he felt it would have been better to have presented no homework and have taken the cane, than to sacrifice his afternoon. After all, unless he was angry, Father Brophy didn't really cane that hard. His lack of judgment began to rankle.

He returned again to his composition. They had been given three titles to choose from, and he had chosen 'Cruelty to Animals'. The other two were 'My Favourite Television Programmes' and 'Old Age'. No thoughts at all came into his mind on old age, and although he wanted to write about his favourite television programmes, he knew it would be a mistake. Brophy only set titles like that to glean information from them. So by a process of elimination, he had decided upon 'Cruelty to Animals'. This choice was also prompted by the fact that a week earlier they had listened to a tape on the subject. Much to his surprise, he remembered a good deal of it. He had written,

Some sports are very cruel to animals. The sport of horse jumping has horses jumping very large fences. Sometimes the fence is so high that the horse can't jump it and has to pull up quickly or else it might crash into the fence. Also sometimes the horse hits the fence with its leg and this might damage the horses leg and the horse might have to be put down.

Zoos are also very cruel to animals. Animals that are kept in the zoo are kept in very small cages and they can't move around like they do in the wild. Some animals don't mind being in cages but birds suffer the most because they can't fly very far. Large cats suffer to because they can't run very far in there cages.

Whales are killed to make fancy womens perfume. Animals which have a furry skin are killed to make fur coats. The fur costs a lot of money and only rich people can buy them. Elephants are killed for there tusks to make necklases and ornaments.

Lots of animals are killed in science experiments each year.

He had been going well, but when Brophy had told him to stay in after school, all the enthusiasm went out of his work. He looked at it without interest and, as a gesture of resentment towards Brophy, decided to end it. He wrote, 'And as you can see that man is very cruel to animals in many different ways and I think it is wrong as animals never do anything to hurt us.'

The essay was obviously too short, but it was a safe gesture. Brophy would be content to punish him for his homework and would turn a blind eye to its brevity.

His half-hour of detention was made worse by the fact that he had no company. The homework he had to repeat was a maths one which consisted of working out percentages of given amounts. He found he could handle the percentages when they were whole numbers, but when fractions became involved, he floundered hopelessly. He knew he was still arriving at incorrect answers, but he tried to compensate for his lack of success by presenting the work as neatly as he could. More of his time was spent underlining in red and ensuring a pleasing layout. Father

Brophy had often said he would never punish a boy for stupidity – dishonesty, laziness, maliciousness – these were punishable offences, but never stupidity. Kiernan did not entirely believe Father Brophy, but at this particular time it suited him to pretend he did.

Father Brophy sat at his desk reading a book, seemingly oblivious to his captive. Kiernan could see from its cover that the paperback was not a religious one. The classroom was disturbingly silent and each empty desk reminded him that its usual occupant was enjoying himself elsewhere. But sooner than he could have hoped for, the work was finished. He approached Father Brophy's desk slowly and stood silent and penitent before him. Father Brophy let him stand for about a minute, pretending he wasn't aware of his presence, then gave the homework a cursory inspection before wordlessly indicating that the boy could go.

Walking home through the housing estate, the boy slowly recovered a feeling of well-being. Perhaps the day could still be salvaged – after all it was Monday, and Monday was his favourite television evening. He made a mental list of his intended viewing. That evening, he knew the film was a Clint Eastwood western, and the prospect made him give a little shuffle of pleasure as he walked. On Mondays, too, his parents both went out to the club, and as his older brothers were usually out, he often had the house to himself. He liked Clint Eastwood a lot. There was never much talking and plenty of action in his films. He loved the way he always looked half-asleep until he had to draw his gun. Father Brophy would not approve of Clint Eastwood, but to Kiernan Caffrey there seemed little in the world that the Father did approve of.

He walked on past the row of shops which formed the centre of the estate. Most of their windows were boarded up and their open doors gave no indication as to what was sold inside. Posters and graffiti spewed over every inch of space, last year's names and events overlaid with fresher additions, like so many layers of skin. A dog sniffed round the wheels of a pram. A wire grille swung loosely like a page in a book. A group of women huddled outside the newsagent's, one still in her slippers and clutching a bottle of milk. He saw two of his classmates come out holding single cigarettes they had bought. He was glad he had stopped smoking, and although he still had the odd one occasionally, he only did it to pass himself. His mind went back to the tape he had heard in school about how scientists made dogs inhale cigarette smoke to find out about lung cancer.

Remembering it was Monday, he walked a little quicker. His mother liked to get the tea over early so that she could get ready to go to the club. Thinking of this reminded him that he was hungry. Tea on Monday was never anything much, but he consoled himself by thinking of the television programmes he was going to enjoy. He cut down an entry. As he turned the corner he almost tripped over a figure crouching in at the hedge of one of the gardens. It was a Brit. They stared into each other's faces, but nothing passed between them except the distancing of caution. The boy saw about six others in similar positions ahead of him. At the start it had been different. Some of them had tried to be friendly and would speak, but too many things had happened since then. But except when there was trouble on and the word was out, only the very young children bothered to stone them. Mostly they were just ignored. He adopted an attitude of casual indifference to the soldiers' presence as he walked by, pulling a twig out of a hedge and beginning systematically to shed its leaves. Two of them carried guns for firing plastic bullets as well as their rifles. All the soldiers he passed stared closely at him, but no one said anything and no one stopped him to look into his schoolbag. Then all but the last man stood up and moved out. As he turned round and watched them go, he saw the first soldier covering their exit and observing the length of the entry. His sleeves were rolled up and he had tattoos on both arms. He was chewing gum with exaggerated movements of his mouth and just before he too left, he winked in the boy's direction. The boy turned away and continued to shed leaves.

As he was walking he saw a small green caterpillar on the cuff of his pullover. He stopped and delicately removed it, then rumbled in his pockets for a tin to put it in. Among the clutter of debris produced was nothing suitable, but then he remembered his lunch box. Taking it out of his bag he placed the caterpillar inside. He knew his mother would not be pleased, but he could remove it as soon as he reached home. There was a rifle shot. He wondered if it would be possible to keep it and look after it until it grew into a butterfly. He had nearly been successful the previous year with frogspawn, but something told him that this would be more difficult. From the sound he knew that it had come from an Armalite. He turned and walked back up the entry. When he reached the top his lunch box was almost knocked from his hand by a boy running. It was one of his classmates charging in the direction of the shops.

'They've got a Brit! They've got a Brit!' he shouted breathlessly.

Kiernan sealed the lunch box and, carefully placing it in his bag, followed the boy. A small crowd of youths had gathered already on a little patch of green that faced the shops. There was a soldier lying on the pavement outside the butcher's shop. His helmet had been taken off and his flak jacket flung open. A soldier on his knees cradled the wounded man's head in his lap. Splatters of blood stippled the shop window and a rivulet of red seeped down the pavement towards the gutter. Near by on the pavement a bottle of milk lay broken. The expression on the face of the soldier who was crouched over the wounded man told that he was dying, and would be dead before medical help arrived. The other soldiers stood upright, their faces pale with fear, holding their rifles to their shoulders and moving them from side to side to cover potential vantage spots where the sniper might be hiding. But they knew, just as the crowd knew, that he would be long gone.

The boy watched as the blood reached the edge of the pavement and trickled into the gutter. An old woman stood motionless in a doorway fingering rosary beads. From the interior of the butcher's shop, faces peered through the meat hanging on skewers, but no one came out. The boy noticed that the shot soldier had tattoos on his arms. A priest came running from somewhere – it was Father Brophy. He started to administer the last rites. The soldiers looked at him with suspicion and listened to his words as if he was mouthing some final curse. The boy felt vindicated in his dislike of the priest.

The crowd had increased in numbers now. Some of them began to shout abuse. The boy was worried that Father Brophy would see him, and slowly he slipped through the crowd to its rear. The shouting grew, with people whistling and banging the ground with anything that came to hand. Then, deepening his voice to try to sound like a grown-up, he shouted at the group huddled in front of the shops,

'Go on, die, ya bastard!'

His voice blended with the others and then he turned away. Soon, more Brits would come and they would be angry. It would be better to be indoors when that happened. Besides, it was Monday, his favourite television night, and his mother always liked to get the dinner over early so that she had plenty of time to get ready for the club. As he broke into a run he reminded himself to remove the caterpillar from his lunch box before he left it in the kitchen. He wondered if it would turn into a butterfly.

THE MARTYRS' MEMORIAL

THE FIRE in the lounge had almost burnt itself out, but no one had the initiative or the courage to put more coal on. It was an unspoken rule that only Mrs McComb or one of her senior lieutenants was entitled to perform that important task, and even on a wet holiday afternoon, none of her guests was inclined to dispute it. The embers glowed brightly in the gloom. Grey, salt-laden squalls gusted against the windows, leaving behind changing patterns of rain. He sat on a window ledge and watched the droplets slide into nothingness. On the seafront the lines of coloured lights swayed like skipping ropes. Few people braved the spray-washed pavement. Only an elderly couple sheathed in macs ventured along its length, their heads bowed as if under a weight, and from time to time the probing wind slipped inside their coats and billowed them out like sails. Scudding clouds darkened the remaining blue pockets of sky, and the sea swelled and wallowed in a shifting swirl of grey. In the distance, the white strand was swathed in thickening cloud, barely distinguishable through the gloom. Up in the convent on the cliff tops, two lights burned like the eyes of some watching animal. He turned away with a shiver.

It was only four o'clock and still two hours away from dinner. The dismal weather had driven almost all the residents of the guest house into the sanctuary of the lounge, and despite the fire there was a cosy feeling of security, as they sheltered like ships in a harbour. The room was furnished with an ill-matching assort-ment of armchairs and settees, unified only by the presence of puffed-up cushions, with gaudy floral covers. A stern, yellow-keyed piano stood to attention against the back wall and a mixture of badly painted pictures and religious texts decorated the walls. Above the fireplace was a photograph of Mrs McComb and the late Mr McComb on their wedding day. He looked round at the dozen or so residents. He knew them by name. They were the same middle-aged and elderly couples who stayed the same time each year, booking the last week of July in order to miss the crowded Twelfth fortnight. Creatures of habit. Mr Cranston sat slumbering on the settee with one of Mrs McComb's edifying religious tomes opened at random on his knee, while his wife knitted somnolently in the same colour of wool she had used the year before. Her eyes had a glazed, faraway expression, and the click of her needles and the rustle of turning pages were the only sounds in the room. Mrs Kilfedder was engrossed in the pages of the *People's Friend*, while her husband, a fisherman from Kilkeel, sat bolt upright in a stiff-backed chair, his arms folded. From time to time, he would close one eye and squint intently into space with the other, as if making mysterious assessments and calculations. He wore a stiff white collar and a tartan tie, open sandals, and a brown Aran cardigan that smelled of fish. The Mehargs, who owned a shoe shop in Ballymena, were having some sort of silent argument, conducted by sharp, bird-like movements of the head and meaningful glances, that finally resolved itself and settled into frosted stares. Close to the fire, Mr and Mrs Gillespie, the retired missionaries, dozed contentedly. After supper each evening, Mrs Gillespie would play the piano which stoutly refused to wilt under the weight of photographs, framed catering certificates and brass ornaments that squatted on its lid, and Mr Gillespie would lead the assembled company in chorus singing. Mrs McComb herself would grace the occasion with her presence, and sing passionately and sincerely.

His own parents puzzled over a jigsaw that they had spread out on a coffee table, and as he watched them he felt a little resentful of their relaxed contentment, and conscious of his own boredom. When he was younger it had been all right, but there was a limit to how many times you could play pitch and putt, walk the cliff path, attend the beach mission. All of it bored him now, but though he wanted something fresh, there seemed little prospect of any change in their predictable holiday pattern. They seemed to genuinely enjoy their annual holiday and looked forward to it with an eager anticipation that left him bemused. It didn't seem to matter about bad weather or anything else – a week in Mrs McComb's Portstewart guest house was, for them, a restorative, a panacea for tired spirits, and a vital preparation for the coming winter. As much as he disliked the prospect, it seemed selfish to spoil it for them in any way.

Outside, the rising wind rattled the windows, and caused the residents to raise their heads.

'Stormy weather ahead,' observed Mr Kilfedder.

'Brewing up all day,' added Mrs Kilfedder, in support of her husband's expert assertion.

'It has got very dark,' said Mrs Cranston timidly, temporarily pausing from her knitting. 'It's like the middle of winter.'

'The darkest hour always comes before the dawn,' said Mr Gillespie, and the profundity of the observation momentarily silenced the outbreak of conversation.

'Yesterday was a nice day,' ventured Mrs Cranston, resuming her knitting, 'though it did get a bit cold later on.'

'At least it was dry,' agreed his mother, holding up a piece of puzzle. 'We walked round to the strand in the afternoon, and it was very pleasant – wasn't it, John?'

'Very pleasant,' confirmed his father. 'The wind was quite fresh, but sure, that's the best thing in the world for blowing away the cobwebs and clearing your brain.'

'You're not far wrong there. Nothing like a good sea breeze in your face for making a man think straight,' said Mr Kilfedder. 'It's when a gale blows up and you're a long way from shore – that's when you start to worry.' And he closed one eye tightly and slowly nodded his head in affirmation.

'That's when the power of prayer can become very real,' said Mr Gillespie. 'I've always found that throughout my life.'

'Amen,' interjected Mrs Gillespie.

'You know, Mr Kilfedder,' he continued, 'we, too, have spent our lives on the high seas of life, fishing – fishing for men. All our lives trawling and netting lost and perishing souls.'

'The young men are all using this radar business now for catching. They didn't need no fancy machines when I was a spindle of a boy on my first boat, and I'll not be using any now. You can have all the fancy gadgets you like, but you'll never replace this,' and he closed both eyes and touched the side of his nose with his finger.

'Smell?' asked Mrs Cranston. 'You smell the fish?'

'Instinct,' growled Mr Kilfedder, and he glared at her with round, wide eyes, as if he had just sighted a mermaid.

'You know,' said Mr Gillespie, a lifetime of experience telling him that an opening had presented itself, 'it reminds me of that story in the Bible where the disciples had been fishing all night and hadn't caught a single fish, and then Jesus appeared and told them where to cast their net. And when they did it, the net was full to overflowing, and you know, we all have to listen to the voice of God guiding us, and follow where he leads us.'

'When you got the call to the mission field,' asked one of the other guests, 'did you know at once it was the voice of God?'

'I would be less than truthful, Miss Penny, if I told you I didn't have doubts at first. The sacrifice involved was so great that it was easy to think of excuses, but just like Samuel, God called again, and there could be no hiding from His voice. And because we heeded that call all those years ago, God has seen fit to bless our lives and bless our work.'

'Amen,' said Mrs Gillespie.

'Amen,' echoed Mrs Meharg.

There was no further conversation, and the guests resumed their previous activities. There was still an hour before dinner. He looked out and saw that it seemed to have stopped raining. Down on the front, a woman was walking a small dog, and two young boys were trying to splash each other in a puddle. The sky was ominously dark, but a little patch of brightness was struggling to emerge and, taking advantage of the lull in conversation, he slipped out of the lounge and down the stairs towards the front door. The curdling smell of cabbage enveloped him and he screwed up his face in miserable anticipation. He hated cabbage, but he knew his mother would expect him to eat at least some of it out of politeness. The one thing he hated worse than Mrs McComb's food was the way the smell of each meal wafted its way up from the depths of the kitchen and permeated every nook and cranny throughout the entire house. Even in his tiny attic with the sloping ceiling, he woke each morning to the sizzling, frizzling smell of soda bread and potato farls. It was strange – even after he had been back home for a few days, the cloying, yellow smell would stay with him and cling to his clothes. As he passed the dining room door, he saw the new girl laying the tables. She was too intent on placing knives and forks to hear his light-footed step.

He crossed the road and clambered down on to the glistening rocks. The tide was going out and the rock pools were brimming lagoons awash with fronds of podded seaweed. Damp black, leathery strands latticed the rocks and purple clots of anemones clung to the shiny solidity of stone. Insects skimmed the film scumming the surface of the water, and he plopped a pebble into the middle of a deep pool and watched the effects of the ripples. Finding a bit of driftwood, he poked under the rubbery mass of coiled tresses, prising them up on the end of the stick before dropping them again. From under some stones he had dislodged, a crab scuttled for new shelter, disguising its destination with a clouded sandstorm of panic, but he did not pursue it. The sky was growing dark and, throwing the stick in the direction of the sea, he stood up and stared with fretful fascination at the convent on the cliff top. There were more lights on now, and he wondered what went on behind those forbidding walls. Crouching down in a cleft in the rocks he peered cautiously at its impervious heart. It struck him suddenly and forcefully that just as he watched it, perhaps someone, somewhere in the maze-like multiplicity of rooms, might at that very moment have him fixed in a fierce and inscrutable gaze. He ducked below the top of the rock and squatted with his back pressed against the cold and crusted surface. Approaching footsteps on the shingle made him start, and with his heart beating fast, he made himself small and silent. Sharp, whorled limpets burrowed into his back and dampness seeped into the seat of his trousers, but he continued to press himself into the rock until the footsteps had trailed away.

That night, Mrs McComb's dinner gong seemed to thunder out its summons even more loudly than usual. He faced the meal with grim determination and did the best he could under his mother's sharp surveillance. Their table was served by Rosemary, the new girl. She was not much older than he was and a little nervous, especially when she carried in the transparent soup that each evening bore a different name, but she managed everything without mishap and he noticed that she smiled a lot. She was slightly smaller than he was and had wiry black hair, pulled back into a bristling ponytail and fixed with a red bow. There was something about the way she walked that intrigued him, but he couldn't understand what it was. He thought she was pretty in a strange sort of way, and he felt an affinity with her, born of a shared youthfulness surrounded by universal senility. But he did not look directly at her, and knew he played no part in her world. As a token of friendship, however, he forced himself to eat more of the cabbage than he could normally have managed, and told himself it didn't taste so bad.

That night, as he lay in his iron-framed, jangling bed under a sloping ceiling, the smell of dinner lingered all about. The bed itself bore a weighty canopy of quilt, sheets and blankets that seemed designed to smother and suffocate the occupant. Sometimes, when he pulled the clothes back, he would find long, thin, brown feathers fluffing across the sheet like giant caterpillars. The first night he had folded the quilt and placed it in the shadowy cavernous wardrobe that smelled of mothballs, and where skinny metal hangers vibrated like wind chimes, but the following morning he had found it returned to its original position. Mrs McComb's guest house ran on very firm rules, and in case anyone might be unsure of what these rules were, they could be found in numerous locations about the house, typed and Sellotaped into place, the favourite one being the backs of doors. Restrictions, injunctions, exhortations bedecked these sites like miniature flags. To sit on the toilet was to read that no cigarette ends or bits of cardboard should be deposited in it, to borrow a book from the bookcase was to be subjected to conditions more strict than any library. To open or close your bedroom door was to read the most copious of scripts. It made him feel as if he was under constant suspicion, as if he was always being watched and that he possessed a dubious, untrustworthy character which might suddenly explode into wild acts of vandalism or arson. It irritated him. Sometimes, when he was really fed up, he almost felt tempted to perform some wild, lawless act, but it was not in his nature – he knew that.

When he had been younger, the holidays in Portstewart had been exciting adventures but it was different now. He had outgrown them – that was all. Nothing ever changed – even the people were familiar, coming back year after year with the same suitcases and raincoats, saying the same things, telling the same jokes. He supposed it was this very familiarity that attracted them. They knew in advance what they would encounter, and Mrs McComb's strict ship and evangelical atmosphere prevented the unwelcome intrusion of unsuitables – the late-night drinkers, the loud Belfast riff-raff, the wrong sort. And anyway, those types were more at home with the entertainments of Portrush. His mother talked about these as if they were the fleshpots of Babylon.

He lay flat on his back and stared at the skylight. In some other room someone coughed huskily. The plumbing gurgled and sucked vociferously, then gargled its ancient throat before falling still again. A toilet flushed and faraway cisterns groaned with the burden of use. Finding it difficult to sleep, he opened the drawer of his bedside cabinet and took out the book he had borrowed from the lounge library. It was a copy of Foxe's *Book of Martyrs* and he lay on top of the bedclothes and turned the pages with grim fascination. He had been reading it for three days, and the horror of it gripped him. As always, he looked at the drawings first of all: *Inquisitors arresting suspected heretic lady*, *The inquisition hall of torture*, *William Hunter, the young martyr*. He pored over the pages, studying the morbid scenes intently, then continued reading. Two passages in particular held a gruesome attraction:

He was of a fine and manly form, and possessed a strong and healthy constitution which served to render his death extremely painful, for he was observed to live an unusual time among the flames. He, however, sang till his aspiring soul took its flight, as in a fiery chariot, from earth to heaven.

'A fiery chariot'. His mind played with the words and his imagination pictured the terrible scene. He read on about another martyr.

On December 14th 1417, he was suspended by chains to a gallows and a fire being kindled under him, he died in the most exquisite and prolonged agony, amidst the imprecations of the priests and monks, who used their best endeavours to prevent the people encouraging him by their prayers.

He read the passage again and again, trying to understand what the phrase 'exquisite and prolonged agony' meant, but he could find no answer. The most unspeakable cruelties screamed at him from the yellowing pages. Unbelievable examples of persecution poured from them, but the names and dates reminded him that he was not reading fiction but historical fact. He marvelled at the unquenchable faith of these martyrs who endured death itself rather than bow the knee to idolatry. He read until his eyes became heavy with sleep, and his mind could take no more of flaming torches and burning flesh. Putting the book back carefully in the drawer, he got ready for sleep, but before he did so, he crept to the window and peered at the darkness on the cliff top that was punctuated only by scattered squares of yellow light. What diabolical schemes were being hatched at that very moment behind its fortified walls, what terrible perversions were being practised in the dark innermost chambers? He shivered, then dived for the safety of the bed, and for once was glad to pull the quilt up under his chin.

That night, he dreamed strange and terrible things. Chanting processions of hooded monks marched slowly up the stairs of Mrs McComb's guest house, hammered down his door and denounced him as a heretic. Then, bound with chains to the stake, wood was piled high around him. All about him distorted faces screamed and clawed as they brandished torches in the darkness, and then from the shadows emerged a purple-robed Papal inquisitor, whose face bore a strange resemblance to that of Mr Gillespie, demanding that he recant and embrace the one true faith. But, calling on God's grace, he steadfastly and resolutely refused, asking God to receive his spirit. Then with hideous cries, the monks rushed forward and thrust their torches into the wood, shooting crimson flames into the frenzied blackness. As the flames raged about him, the scene faded to be replaced by other nightmares, each one more terrible than the last and filled with fetters, burning brands and black-masked inquisitors.

When the morning came, he felt so drained and unsettled that he resolved to return the book and not open its pages again. And anyway, the whole thing was silly, an episode from history that bore no relation to the present. Catholics were Catholics, and while not exactly blood brothers, they were hardly liable to burn you in oil just because you were a Protestant, or stretch you on the rack in an attempt to convert you. Certainly, they weren't to be trusted, but that didn't mean that behind their walls sinister plots were being hatched to ensnare unsuspecting Protestants out on their holidays. But then again, if their Pope wasn't exactly the anti-Christ, it was undeniable that they practised strange and unnatural rituals like worshipping statues and praying to the Virgin Mary, and if even only half the things they said about what the priests and nuns got up to were true, well, then, you could never tell. There was, too, something about that convent on the hill that unsettled him. Squatting on the cliffs, overlooking the sea, it had the fortified look of a castle, and there was an eerie silence shrouding it that never faltered or revealed even the slightest clue of what went on inside. It was like a secret that you always wanted to know but were never told.

At breakfast, optimism prevailed about the possibility of good weather. Mr Meharg had listened to the weather forecast on his little transistor and a clear dry day had been predicted, but Mr

Kilfedder, on the evidence of an early morning stroll, was more sceptical.

'When you've been reading the weather as long as I have, you learn to read the signs. You see things that the untrained eye would miss. I felt rain in the air.'

'We'll be sure to carry our macs,' said Mrs Meharg appreciatively. 'Some of those showers can be very heavy.'

His mother and father discussed the possible options for the day, and asked for his opinion, but when he suggested going into Portrush, his father said they should save that for a wet day, and his mother nodded her head in forceful agreement. And so the day followed the pattern of the previous days, and he tagged along, doggedly unenthusiastic. They inspected the harbour, played putting, had sausage rolls in a café for lunch, an ice-cream in Morelli's, and plied the long path to the strand. Later that afternoon, they were invited by the Gillespies to attend a valedictory service in Dunseverick Baptist Church, and after dinner they set off in their green Morris Minor. Only after repeated assurances about his safety and general well-being had his parents been persuaded to leave him behind. Mr Gillespie had seemed slightly offended, but his mother had made some excuse on his behalf and, with a farewell kiss and comb of his hair, they rather reluctantly left him behind. She had left a suggested programme of activity for the evening, and he had reassured her with a submissive and co-operative spirit. The prospect of an evening's freedom did not immediately fill him with exhilaration but unchaperoned independence was a novelty to him and he felt he should not waste it. So, after dutifully waving off his parents, he sat down on the iron seat outside the guest house and considered the limited options available to him. While he was doing this, the front door opened and the new girl came and stood in the doorway. Looking sideways at her, he realised that she hadn't noticed him, but although he thought of speaking, he could come up with nothing to say. She seemed to be standing breathing in the air, and it was some time before she became aware of his presence.

'It's so hot in that kitchen, sometimes you think you're going to melt,' she said, smiling at him.

He smiled self-consciously back at her, but still could not think of anything to say. He noticed she had a green bow in her hair and her face was flushed. A wisp of her black, wiry hair flicked rebelliously across her forehead.

'Are you waiting for your parents?' she asked.

'No, they've gone off to some meeting. I managed to get out of it.'

'Lucky you,' she said, still smiling. 'Nobody should have to sit in meetings on their holidays. What're you going to do?'

'I haven't decided yet . . . I'm not really sure.'

There was a pause in the conversation. He watched her push the wayward wisp of hair back into place. Somewhere inside himself, he could feel a strange sensation bubbling. He struggled frantically for something sensible to say.

'Do you like working for Mrs McComb?' he asked.

She looked back over her shoulder cautiously, smiled and said, 'It's not too bad,' but then stepped off the doorstep and sat down on the seat beside him and whispered, 'It's terrible, really. You have to get up at the crack of dawn and she stands and supervises you from morning to night, just hoping you'll make some mistake.'

He felt instinctive sympathy for her, but did not know the words to convey it.

'You weren't here last year,' he said.

'No, this is my first summer job. I'm not sure if it's worth the money or not. I can't make up my mind. But you don't seem to be enjoying yourself much either.'

'We come here every year and it's all right, but I'm a bit fed up with it. It gets boring being with your parents all the time.'

'We're both prisoners of Mrs McComb!' she whispered in a melodramatic voice, her eyes wide and round.

They laughed, and their laughter forged a bond of friendship. A silence settled again, and his eyes fixed on a far-off yacht. He was thinking that he wished they could both get on it and sail away, but it wasn't the type of thing you could say to a girl you'd only just met, and he tried to stop himself thinking it, just in case his thoughts were somehow readable.

'My name's Rosemary,' she said.

'I know,' he replied sheepishly.

'What's yours?' she asked.

'Martin,' and as he answered, he had a terrible suspicion that his face was turning a bright shade of red.

'Have you decided what you're going to do tonight, Martin?'

'No, not yet. I might go fishing.' He didn't know why he had said it, because until that second, the idea had never entered his head, and in any case, he didn't have so much as a piece of string in the way of fishing equipment.

'Oh, fishing,' she said. 'They're showing a film in the cinema. I was thinking of going. It's *The Swiss Family Robinson*.'

Immediately, he regretted making up the story about fishing.

'*Swiss Family Robinson* – that sounds interesting. Is it starting soon?'

'In half an hour. It's just down the front.'

He shuffled nervously on the seat, but the situation was uncomfortably new to him, and his apprehension was greater than his courage. Words faltered to the end of his tongue, his lips shaped to form them, but they slipped away into silence. Out at sea, the yacht had disappeared. She looked at him quizzically, then smiled.

'Would you like to come and see it?'

'Yes, I would,' he gulped, and his heart raced across the blue ocean that danced before his eyes.

'I'll meet you here in ten minutes,' she said, smiling again, then she hurried off into the guest house.

He grasped the cold iron struts of the seat in an effort to reassure himself that he hadn't imagined what had just happened. His heart was still skipping, but slowly he felt himself in the grip of another emotion, that of fear. What had he just done? He had never been out with a girl before in his whole life – he didn't have the first idea of what you were supposed to say, never mind what you were supposed to do. He would make a complete fool of himself, he would make a complete mess of it, be totally ridiculous. And his parents! Going out with a girl he had only just met had definitely not been included in his mother's programme of suggested activities. The pictures! As well as never having been out with a girl, he had never been inside a cinema. They didn't even have a black-and-white television set at home. Going to the pictures was considered by his parents to be something vaguely sinful, and certainly not conducive to godliness. On the only occasion he had sought permission to go, it had been refused, and when he had asked for a reason, his mother had talked about the ungodly life style of film stars, and if the world was to end, how would he feel if God was to find him sitting in a cinema? Not really knowing how the mind of God worked, he had made no comment on the second reason, but argued that his parents didn't satisfy themselves on the private morality of the butcher before they bought lamb chops from him, or the baker before they bought a loaf of bread. But his mother had absolutely brought an end to the argument and he had never asked again. If going to the pictures wasn't exactly a first division sin, it was still something to abstain from, on a par with smoking and dancing. He would definitely have to lie to them about his evening's activity, even if *The Swiss Family Robinson* was hardly liable to corrupt anyone. Indeed, didn't his own father have a copy in his bookcase, and if it was all right to read, then it had to be all right to watch.

Wetting the palms of his hands, he plastered down hair at the crown of his head that had been sticking up since his nightmare-torn sleep, checked that he had an adequate supply of money, and wet some of the scuff marks on his sandals to darken them. The front door opened and he stood up, but it was Mr and Mrs Kilfedder who came out, and he mumbled a greeting and then sat down again.

'All on your own?' asked Mrs Kilfedder. 'Would you like to come out with us?'

'Thanks very much, but I'm thinking of going fishing,' he lied, his face colouring and panic rising in him that they would stay and talk to him until she arrived. But Mr Kilfedder seemed in a hurry to be off, and, closing the front gate, they set off at a brisk pace.

He looked at his watch – she was late. Perhaps she had changed her mind, maybe Mrs McComb had found her more work to do. As the minutes ticked by, he was certain that she wasn't coming, and a feeling of relief washed over him. Then, just as he was reconsidering what he should do, the front door opened again and she bounced up to him.

She was wearing a white cardigan over a white blouse and light blue trousers. Her hair was brushed and pulled back tightly from her face into a ponytail. He thought she was wearing some make-up, but he wasn't sure. He stood up and smiled at her.

'Shall we go?' she asked.

As they walked the short distance to the cinema, he felt more self-conscious than at any time in his life. He wanted to be with her very much, but he felt conspicuous and suffered from the uncomfortable feeling that everyone was staring at them. They walked together, but not closely, and as he looked about with simulated casualness, he hoped people would think she was his sister. She was talking to him, but he felt so confused that he was sure he was babbling gibberish in reply. He avoided the gaze of passers-by and felt imaginary eyes burning holes in his back. They reached the cinema and he knew he had to pull himself together. Pretend experience – he decided that was the key to success, but when confronted by a list of meaningless areas of seating, he was momentarily thrown, until he asked her where she would like to sit. He insisted on paying for them both, then followed her as she led him to their seats, and in the more private world of the cinema, he felt a little less conspicuous. The slightly sinful aura that surrounded the experience lent it a tantalisingly criminal quality that produced damp pools in the palms of his hands and left his senses alert and expectant.

The film was about to start, so there was little opportunity for further conversation, and as they settled stiffly into their seats, the only contact was where the points of their elbows touched on the arm rest. He suddenly felt different without being exactly sure how. Was it reckless, adventurous, even adult? He wasn't sure, but he began to think that he liked the feeling. And then, in a moment he knew would stay with him for the rest of his life, he watched the film begin. His mouth opened wide in wonder, and he could feel an idiotic grin spreading across his whole face – the screen was huge, a more vast stretch of colour than he could ever have imagined, and the colours so intensely immediate that they seemed to reach out and draw him into a glorious Technicolor world. The delicious dark cocooned them and funnelled their vision towards a world more tangible than the real world itself. Blue tropical seas ringed white-beached coral islands, so real he wanted to stretch out his hand and touch. Portstewart, Mrs McComb, his parents – all faded from his consciousness as he breathed in the living world of the screen. He was aware of only one other person, and that was the girl who sat quiet and still by his side, their only contact being the light touch of their elbows.

As the drama unfolded, he imagined himself protecting her from raging storms at sea, charging wild animals, swarms of cutlass-carrying pirates; building a house with logs and vines, and not wanting ever to be rescued from their island. He looked at her discreetly, but she seemed intent on the film, and then he started to feel a little foolish. She would laugh at him if she knew what nonsense he was thinking – she was probably laughing at him already. Then just at that moment, the high drama gave way to heart-rending pathos, and his heart clanged like a cathedral bell as he felt her hand slip into his. He glanced at her, but she still stared straight ahead at the film. He clasped the small warmth of her hand, and his whole being vibrated with excitement, and he marvelled that sin could taste so sweet. He wanted to put his arm around her, but he did not dare, and his tingling soul hoped that the film would never end. But he knew it could not be so, and, when all too soon the final credits rolled and the house lights came on, their hands slipped apart.

'Did you like the film?' she asked.

'It was great,' he replied enthusiastically, 'and a lot better than fishing.'

As they filed out of the dark cinema, the brightness of the summer evening hurt his eyes and they both seemed a little unsure of where they were going, but with growing self-confidence, he bought her an ice-cream cone in Morelli's and then, crossing the road, they walked along the front. He felt a little less self-conscious now, and as they drew level with the guest house, he hoped the evening wasn't over. They both paused and looked up at the uninviting facade.

'Would you like to walk round to the strand, Rosemary?'

'That would be nice – it's too early to go indoors.'

They strolled on, licking the cones, and he hoped above everything that he didn't have a white ring around his mouth. He found it easier to talk now, and he asked her questions about what it was like to work for Mrs McComb.

'She calls the guests "the locusts" because she thinks you eat so much. "Rosemary," she'll say, "ring the dinner gong and summon the locusts." And after you're all gone, she'll survey the empty tables and say something like, "The locusts didn't leave much tonight," and – never leave anything on your plate – because you're bound to get it back again as part of something else.'

They both giggled. He liked it when she laughed. He wished he could say funny things that would amuse her.

'No one in the kitchen's allowed to cut anything except her. It doesn't matter what it is – meat, cake, bread, ice-cream – she does the cutting. That's why the portions are so small. You want to see her do it. She stares at it and weighs it up like she was about to shear a sheep, and then she goes to it – never makes a mistake either, always gets the exact number of pieces needed. You know, too, the way you can always hear something jangling when she walks – well, it's the keys of the pantry, she never lets them out of her sight.'

'What I hate most is all those signs telling you all the things you're not supposed to do. Even though you'd never thought of doing them, when you see them, it makes you feel like doing them anyway – if you know what I mean.'

She nodded her head and he felt she understood.

'What do you think of Mr and Mrs Gillespie?' he asked.

'If you promise not to tell anyone, I could tell you a few secrets about them two holy Joes. Do you know what she wears in bed?'

He shook his head and his imagination raced wildly, creating all kinds of improbably exotic images.

'Woollen bedsocks and a nightcap! And every night I have to put a hot water bottle in their bed because she can't stand the cold. Says she's never been warm since she came home from Africa, and he has to have porridge each morning for his breakfast, and the milk has to be lukewarm. Not like Mr Kilfedder now – he sleeps with the window open every night and all his clothes have this fishy smell.'

He listened with devoted interest, enjoying the light, skipping lilt of her talk, and glad that he did not have to carry the burden of instigating conversation. They walked along the path that twisted between the sea and the convent wall, and although he looked up at its windows, it held no threat or menace for him. Down below, the sea rushed into the narrow eddies and channels thrust out at it by the black, sharp-edged rocks and shot salted spray towards them. In a moment of impulsive daring, he took her hand in his and waited, sensitive to the slightest sign that her hand did not welcome his, but none came, and he walked on, hoping the sea breeze would drain the redness out of his face. When voices announced the approach of other walkers, he would drop her hand gently, then retake it discreetly after they had passed. Reaching a wooden seat, they stopped, and sitting down, watched the sea surging in. Neither of them spoke, and the only sound was the throaty slap and hiss of the waves as they broke below them. He rested his back against the stone wall and wondered what she was thinking. His eyes focused on a squat door set deep in the wall. He had never noticed it before.

'I always think that place is really creepy,' he said.

'What place?'

'In there, the convent,' he replied, nodding his head in its direction.

'That's where I go to school,' she said, with laughter in her voice.

'Where you go to school?' He didn't understand.

'I go to the convent school,' she said, looking at him.

'You mean – you're a . . . ' he stammered.

'I'm a Catholic,' she said, smiling at him. 'Does it make any difference?'

'No, no difference,' he said, dropping her hand as if it had become a hot pincer, and wondering if he should dive head-first into the foaming depths below. He must have been blind. He stared at her eyes for confirmation of her religion, and remembered he had always thought there was something funny about the way she walked. Oh, yes, the signs were all there as clear as day. He had really done it now. His memory flicked desperately through his mother's copious catechism on Catholicism – 'You can never trust them', 'loyal to the half-crown but not the crown', 'ruled by Rome' – until he reached the relevant one. He struggled to remember the exact words, but it was something about them having ways of tricking you into marriage and the priests always getting the children. What did she mean, 'ways of tricking you'? Why did she always have to be so vague?

'Do you like the school?' he asked, desperately stalling for time, until he could think of an escape route. At any second that squat door could burst open and a predatory procession of priests and nuns would lay hold of him and whisk him inside those high walls from where no future trace of him would ever emerge. He had been duped. His gullibility had led him there like a lamb to the slaughter. Guilt, too, seeped into his soul. Roaring flames had failed to extract life-saving compromise from the likes of Latimer and Ridley, and here was he with his bag already packed and halfway down the road to Rome, enticed by a pair of blue eyes and a friendly smile. Some martyr he'd make – they wouldn't even need to show him the rack. How was he to make his escape? He looked again at the door, but there was no sign of it opening, or of his nightmare becoming reality. He tried to appear normal, and a little curiosity filtered into his initial panic.

'Do they try to get you to become nuns?' he asked.

'Nuns!' she laughed. 'No, they do not, and a right nun I'd make. Can you imagine me in a nun's habit?'

He admitted to himself that he couldn't.

'Are there statues and things like that in the classrooms?' he asked.

'Where did you hear all this stuff? The classrooms are just classrooms with blackboards and desks and things.'

The way she said this made him feel a little foolish. He stared out at the sea. The door had still not opened. Perhaps it wasn't going to.

'Rosemary, Mrs McComb's a Protestant and I thought because you worked for her you were too,' he ventured uncertainly.

'Mrs McComb will employ anyone who'll accept the little she pays them. Anne's a Catholic as well. It's funny, though – she puts a tract in each of our wage envelopes every Friday night.'

He couldn't help smiling. He had decided that the door was not going to open. They sat in silence for a moment. It was getting colder now, and the sea looked restless and troubled. What should he do? Then he felt her small hand take his again, and it was still full of warmth as it rested there like some tiny bird pulsing with life. He held on to it and did not let it go. Out at sea a light flashed. She snuggled against his side, but already his parents were looming large in his thoughts, and soon it would be time for them to return. He had to get away, he had to go back. He knew he had to tell her. There could be no putting it off any longer, and he turned his face gently towards her.

'Rosemary . . . I have to . . . I want to . . .'

But his courage failed him, his pursed lips freezing in silence, and then, to his alarm, he saw a tightly pursed pair of lips moving towards his own. She had misunderstood. He closed his eyes in the face of this terrible and unavoidable collision. And then her small, compelling mouth found his, and pressed hotly against it, shooting an electric shock through his senses. His heart vibrated more loudly than Mrs McComb's dinner gong – he had never known anything could be so agonising and so wonderful, and about ten million other things at the same time.

They pulled apart, and then, closing his eyes, he kissed her on the side of her nose before his mouth found hers again, and he felt as if he was on that orchid-drenched tropical island, or drowning in some coral sea. What did it feel like? How could he describe it? He kissed her again, more slowly this time, like a scientist conducting an experiment, savouring the sensation and searching for words to help him understand what it was he felt, and then his memory took him back to something he had read, and as his lips explored, he remembered the words. 'Exquisite and prolonged agony.' That was it – that was what it meant, that was what it felt like in the heart of the kiss. He performed the experiment again.

Dusk was falling now, and without speaking, they both knew it was time to return. They walked back slowly, hand in hand, and neither of them spoke very much, and it felt to him almost as if words were no longer necessary. Suddenly, they were aware of someone coming towards them, but they made no attempt to hide their friendship, and he held on to her hand proudly. It was Mr Kilfedder on a pre-supper stroll, reluctant to go indoors until his prophecy of rain was proved accurate. As he drew level with them, he closed one eye and surveyed them critically.

'Well, Martin, you seem to have landed a very good catch,' he said, wryly, and then he marched stoutly on in search of dark clouds.

After he was gone they both giggled, trying to suppress their laughter until he was out of sight.

'Do you think he'll tell your parents?' she asked.

'I don't think so, and anyway, it doesn't matter,' he replied, with unaccustomed recklessness.

They parted at the front door of the guest house, and as he watched her disappear into the secret depths of the kitchen, he decided that he liked the way she walked. His mother and father were already in the lounge, and while he knew she would want a full account of his activities, he felt a new spirit of audacity budding inside himself that left him unmoved by the threat of censure or punishment. And so, when his mother enquired how he had spent his time, he stated with casual indifference that he had been fishing and when, with some scepticism, she asked what he had used for tackle, he enigmatically and somewhat pleasurably replied, 'Radar.' The clanging chords of Mrs McComb's solemn piano forestalled further investigation, and although he knew the inquisition would resume in the morning, the prospect held no fear for him. Mrs Gillespie had commenced her evening session of communal choruses and so no further questions were possible, but as soon as the recital was ended, and before the brass ornaments had finished trembling, he announced that he was retiring for the evening. His departure evoked a confused protest from his mother and a bemused smile from his father, and he knew that he would be the subject of discussion during the remainder of the evening, and the target for a more thorough appraisal tomorrow, but as he mounted the brass-rodded stairs to his room with the sloping ceiling, he gave no further thought to the morning, for he had much to reflect upon.

Folding up the flapping quilt, he pitched it on top of the wardrobe with a flourish, then studied himself in the clouded mirror. Slightly to his surprise, he could detect no apparent change in his physical appearance and yet, in some indefinable way, he did feel different.

As he lay on top of the jangling, squeaking bed, he considered how a day that started off so dully had ended with the most momentous of memories. He had seen his first film, he had been kissed for the first time – he would not easily forget either – and his holiday was not yet over. Who knew what other adventures stretched ahead of him? But in that moment of triumph, some-where in the back of his mind a little flag of self-doubt, edged with guilt, began to flutter. He looked at the bedside drawer where Latimer, Ridley and Cranmer smouldered accusingly, and he could hear their voices uniting in condemnation. Had he betrayed them?

He stared up at the shadowy square of skylight, and listened to the whispers of the house. He was struggling to remember something, something his mother had said. Something about Catholics. With intense concentration, he flicked again through the pages of her catechism, trying to find what he was looking for. It was something about the feelings they should have towards Catholics.

And then at last it came back to him, the exact words she had used – 'We must love them individually, even though we hate their religion.' That was it – her exact words, 'love them indi-vidually'.

He lay back on the bed and smiled. It was the end of a memorable day. He had seen his first film, he had kissed his first girl, he had kept the faith; and as water gurgled and danced in the pipes, he looked again at the flickering skylight and felt his soul take flight, as in a chariot of fire, from earth to the starry heavens.

THE APPRENTICE

IT WAS very important to get the time right. Looking at the watch he had borrowed secretly from his sister, he saw that he was much too early. His anxiety to prove his reliability had prompted him to set out at least an hour too soon. Being early was both dangerous and foolish and would draw unwelcome attention. He looked at the watch again and knew he could not go to the spot marked out for him. Swinging his red sports bag into a more comfortable position on his shoulder, he allowed himself a glance at the open iron gate, then turned back the way he had come.

The afternoon was cold and he cupped his hands together in front of his mouth and blew warm breath into them. He wished he had worn his gloves. There were plenty of people about but he drifted from shop window to shop window without making eye contact with anyone. He turned up the black fur collar of his green jacket. Out of the corner of his eye, he saw a face he recognised, and huddled in a doorway until it had passed. He looked at the watch again and, unwilling to believe that only a few minutes had passed since his last glance, held it up to his ear and listened to its ticking. He had to put in time and he needed to do a better job than he was doing at that moment. There was a second-hand bookshop at the corner and he opened the door and went in. Thousands of second-hand paperbacks were stacked on makeshift shelves, classified into a multitude of subjects. Some of them looked ancient, their prices marked in old money and smelling musty and dead. Others were newish with garish covers where half-naked girls draped themselves over dishevelled beds or stroked the barrels of guns. Lifting one up, he read the blurb on the back. He thumbed the pages and, staring at the small print, knew it would take him a lifetime to read. There were no pictures, just pages and pages of the same small, black print. He wondered how anyone could be bothered to make such a physical effort and yet he was curious as he watched men browsing intently. He felt as if there was some kind of secret world enclosed between the covers – a world from which he was excluded. Then an elderly man with a small dog entered and deposited half a dozen books on the counter. After inspecting them, the owner of the shop handed over some money. An idea dawned on him. If he could gather up a clatter of books maybe he could make some money for himself. There were bound to be some lying about the house and perhaps he could extract some from school. No one would miss a few. It was a potential variation on lemonade bottles or scrap metal.

Not wanting to stay in the shop too long, he shouldered the bag and went out into the street. Involuntarily, his gaze went towards the iron gate. It was this gaze that prevented him from seeing the approach of one of his classmates. The unexpected sound of his voice made him jump.

'What's up with you, Ricky? Rob a bank or something?'

'I didn't see you coming.'

'You nearly jumped out of your pants. What were you doing in the shop? Looking for porno books?'

Of all the people he could possibly have met, he could think of no one worse than Chick Kierney, but he tried to be calm and bluff it out.

'I was just looking around.'

'Books are no good – you have to read for ages before you find a good bit. It's not worth the effort. Mags are best. I can get you some if you've got the dough.'

'Naw, I'm not interested, Chick. Anyway, who needs mags when you can have the real thing?'

Chick smiled and thumped him playfully on the shoulder.

'Go on ye boy ye. Now you're talking.'

The conversation could have gone on forever. He had to extract himself. Looking deliberately at his watch, he said he had to go.

'Where're you going? What've you got in your sports bag?'

He silently cursed his classmate's insatiable curiosity, but forced himself into restraint.

'I'm going swimming in the leisure centre. Do you want to come?'

'In this weather? You must be joking. C'mon and we'll go round the town, and pick up a couple of good things.'

'Can't, Chick, I'm meeting someone,' he replied with a tone of finality, then turned and started to move off down the street.

'You're chicken, Ricky-dicky. Don't pee in the pool or you'll turn the water yellow!'

He clenched his fists at the insult, but kept on walking. He would settle that particular score at some later date. Crossing the street, he headed for the sports shop and mingled with the other young window-gazers. His eyes flitted over the expensive football boots and the kits of leading teams. He thought it was a con the way they changed them every year, so that no sooner had you bought your favourite team's kit than it was out of date. It was a racket. If ever he was rich, he would buy everything in the window – it all looked so new and fresh, with that clean, crisp smell that made you want to touch.

He walked on down the street and into the arcade. The smell of a hot dog stand curdled the air and reminded him that he was cold and hungry. Counting the change in his pocket, he found enough to buy one and loaded it with sauce and mustard until it dripped like an ice-cream cornet. He looked at his watch again and saw with some relief that time had started to pass. But it was still too early. Eating the hot dog, he crossed the road and went into the pet shop. Outside on the pavement were aquariums, dog baskets and kennels, a tank full of goldfish and an assortment of cages and equipment for pets. Inside, the fetid smell of animals flowed over him but he was indifferent to it, inspecting the stacked cages of birds in the order he always followed. First the budgerigars, vibrant in blue, yellow and green, then the canaries, zebra finches and Java sparrows. There was a mynah bird he hadn't seen before, and a new pair of lovebirds. White doves rustled and nestled together and he tapped the cage with his finger and cooed gently at them. Then, crouching down on his hunkers, he looked in at the rabbits, their doleful pink eyes staring impassively back at him. Further along were white mice, and breaking off a piece of bread, he fed them through the bars of the cage.

'Don't feed the animals son,' boomed a voice from behind the counter. 'They get fed enough and they don't need any more.'

He stepped back from the cage and stared at the sawdust floor.

'And by the look of that thing, you've probably given them and yourself a good dose of food poisoning.'

Embarrassed by the public chastisement, he sidled slowly up the shop and pretended to be studying a book on hamsters. After what he considered a suitable period of time, he casually ambled out the door and back on to the street. Looking at his watch, he calculated that if he walked slowly and went the long way round, it would be the right time to arrive at the gate. Suddenly a large hand clutched his shoulder.

'Long time no see, Ricky.'

It was James Fallon, the youth club leader. He felt the broad hand drawing him aside, away from the middle of the pavement, the man's height and size overshadowing him and trapping him in the doorway of a closed-down shop.

'Where've you been, Ricky boy? It's not like you to stay away for so long. What's wrong? Did somebody do something to you?'

'It's nothing like that, Mr Fallon. I've been busy recently. I wanted to come, but I wasn't able.'

'And what makes a young buck like you so busy then?'

He had talked himself into a dead-end and his brain scrambled to find some escape.

'Just things – you know how it is.'

'You're a real mystery man, Ricky. Father Logue's been asking after you as well, and the team's missing its centre-forward – we've had three replacements and they haven't scored a goal between them.'

He glanced at the boy's sports bag.

'You're not turning out for someone else, are you?'

'No, I'm going swimming at the leisure centre. I'll be coming back to the club all right. I'll probably be up tomorrow night.'

'That's good, Ricky, that's good. Have you heard from your brother yet?'

He wanted to look at his watch, but knew he could not. He fidgeted nervously from foot to foot, aware that time was moving on. Everything seemed to be going against him.

'He's not great at writing letters Mr Fallon, but we're going up to see him next month.'

'Well, tell him I was asking for him. Maybe I'll get to see him when he's feeling settled.'

'I'll do that. I have to go now because I'm meeting someone at the leisure centre.'

'You're a real busy lad, Ricky. I'll not keep you any longer – I wouldn't want you to be late.'

Smiling gently, he stepped aside, but before the boy could step out on to the pavement, he returned his hand firmly to his shoulder.

'Come back to the club, son. Run the streets and you'll end up in trouble. It's not worth it, Ricky.'

'Don't worry about it. I'm coming back. I'll be up tomorrow night.'

They parted, and as they walked in different directions, he glanced over his shoulder several times to check he wasn't being watched, and then, quickening his pace, he hurried towards the iron gate. Meeting two people he knew had been a piece of bad luck, but he had survived and it was now behind him. Proving himself reliable and trustworthy was all that mattered – he owed it to his brother. People walked past him, their faces pale and pinched with the cold, and he felt apart from them. As an old woman trundled a battered pram towards him, loaded with second-hand clothing, he crossed the road and, without looking right or left, walked through the gate that was a side entrance to the chapel. Once inside, he stepped off the path and stood with his back to the wall where he was unseen from the street. He was nervous now, and glanced repeatedly at his watch, knowing that the fifteen-minute waiting period had started. An old woman came through the gate heading towards the side door of the chapel, but she did not see him. Five minutes passed and no one else entered or left. He shuffled his feet and blew into his hands. Perhaps nothing would happen. Although he would not consciously admit it, part of him wished for the fifteen minutes to pass without his being needed.

His eyes flicked to the couple of stunted trees growing in the grounds of the chapel. They had shed most of their leaves and the few remaining fluttered lifelessly like tattered flags. Above, the sky was a strange blue-grey colour. Around his feet a spume of the previous day's confetti fluttered up in the wind. He looked at his watch again. Suddenly a man appeared at the end of the path – he was early. He tensed in readiness, but there was something wrong – the man was walking unsteadily, swaying from side to side. Something had gone terribly wrong. He felt the press of panic and thought of taking to his heels, but something stronger forced him to wait. By now the man had zigzagged close enough to be seen clearly and the panic was replaced by relief. It was a drunk. He pulled himself back into the shadow of the wall and dropped the sports bag to the ground, but his relief was short-lived. If the drunk had been walking at normal speed he probably would never have seen him, but as he drew close to the gate he stopped, and with flailing co-ordination attempted to light a cigarette.

'Hey son, can you help me a wee minute?'

He swayed off the path and lurched over to him, the smell of booze oozing out of every pore.

'Lend us a few bob, son. I want to light a candle for my wee boy. My wife died last year and now he's having a big operation. The doctors don't know if he'll make it or not.'

At that moment he would have given all the money he had in the world to be rid of this unwanted and dangerous distraction, but he knew without looking that his pockets were hopelessly empty. He had spent the last of his money in the arcade.

'My wee boy's all I've left in the whole world. Just a few bob to light a candle for him.'

The begging had become more insistent, and a shaking hand

wiped away imaginary tears. He knew that he had to do something quickly. As one hand searched deliberately in his pocket,
the other grabbed his bag and he side-stepped the drunk as if
evading a tackle on the soccer field. Hurrying down the path
towards the chapel he heard only a slurred, broken curse pursue
him. Then from a safe distance he turned and watched the man
stagger out through the gate, rehearsing his lines for the next
audience. When he was sure he had gone, he returned to his
original position and waited silently. A glance at his watch told
him there were only five minutes left. Perhaps no one would
come. Perhaps he would not be needed. Four minutes left. He
cupped his hands again and blew into them. Suddenly, he tensed
and tightened his grip on the shoulder bag – a man was running
along the path towards him. A little cloud of breath preceded
him, and by the way the distance between them was closing
rapidly, it was obvious that he was running hard. So this was it.
With a hand that shook a little, he unzipped the bag and held it
open. The man was level with him now but they did not speak or
look into each other's faces. He had stopped running but was still
breathing heavily as he took it out of his pocket and dropped it
into the boy's bag. Then he was gone, out into the street and
away, a blur in the dusk, another face in the crowd. It was smaller
and heavier than he had imagined and it felt warm as he carefully
wrapped it in the towel and zipped up the bag. Then he too was
gone, newly articled and proud, stepping out with the pride a
young man feels on the first day of his first job.

THE CATCH

THE BED confined him like a strait-jacket, each sheet and blanket smothering him with its endless heaviness. He seemed unable to lie in one position for more than a few seconds before a nervous restlessness drove him to seek relief. It had been a mistake to go to bed so early, but he had taken his parents' advice when they told him that a good night's sleep would settle him. If only he could sleep. He closed his eyes tightly and tried to make his mind completely blank, but the more he tried, the more it seemed to flit feverishly from one idea to another.

The whole house was alive with sound. He heard the clink of glasses and his aunt's high-pitched laughter. His mother was ironing his uniform and he hoped she would concentrate on getting his trouser creases really sharp. A pulse of panic suddenly shook him – what would happen if her attention wandered while she was chatting with her sister and burned a hole in them? He sat bolt upright. The whole bed creaked with the sudden movement. But no, he was being foolish, he knew his mother would do those trousers better than she had ever done them. He lay down again. It was a matter of personal pride that her son should be perfectly turned out on such an important occasion. He tried to sleep again, but his uncle's voice droned persistently on. They had emigrated to Canada only five years previously, but now they spoke and acted as if they had lived there all their lives. He smiled when he thought of his uncle's brightly checked trousers and white shoes. When they went down the pub he stood out like a sore thumb.

They were home for three weeks and were staying for each week with a different relation. He wished they could have visited at a different time, as somehow they seemed to distract his attention and put even more pressure on him than there was already. They would be there tomorrow of course. To see 'The Glorious Twelfth' again was one of the reasons they had chosen July. Then a feeling of guilt washed over his irritation. After all, his aunt and uncle had been really good to him when the family had visited them in Toronto the year before. They had travelled with the Maple Leaf Club and it was the most exciting thing he had ever done in his life. He remembered going to the top of the CN Tower and thinking he must be standing at the very top of the world. He had taken a photograph, but it hadn't come out. Then he thought of the cine-camera his uncle had brought with him to film the procession. The thought of everything preserved on film for ever brought back the pulse of panic.

Six months earlier 'The Glorious Twelfth' had filled him with a thrill of expectancy, but as the weeks passed and it loomed nearer he felt increasingly nervous. Now that it was only a sleep away he felt sick with fear. Tomorrow the whole world would be watching as he led 'The Sons of the East' flute band, and with the eye of the universe fixed exclusively on him, he would throw the mace into the air and catch it as it fell. The burden of that knowledge weighed heavily on his shoulders and crushed his spirit, but there could be no escape from the terrible inevitability.

He could catch the mace blindfolded, he could catch it in his sleep. He had practised his routine incessantly during the last few months until his brain no longer needed to tell his fingers what to do. Everyone said he was as good as they had seen, and yet as the day drew nearer, his confidence began to slowly drain away. His mind snatched with mounting alarm at all the things that might go wrong. This was his first Twelfth as leader. He had walked the previous two years as a player. It was his lack of skill as a player that had helped him win the job in the first place. He could never really master the flute, apart from the two or three basic tunes that were the core of the repertoire. The band leader, Mr Morrison, could see that his heart wasn't in it. Just when he had been seriously considering packing it all in, Mr Morrison had called at the house one evening and told him that the regular drum major had found a job in England and the band would need a replacement. He was offering it to him because often during the breaks at practice he had watched him playing around with the mace. Mr Morrison said he had a promising style, and because he knew his father, he was going to give him a trial run. He had jumped at the opportunity and his parents shared his pride when they heard the news.

So far everything had gone well. On their first outings in the marching season he had impressed everyone with his dexterity and style. He copied the basic technique from the more experienced leaders he had watched, and then added a few little frills and fancies of his own. Mr Morrison said that for a fifteen-year-old he showed great composure and had a good future ahead of him. It seemed to come so naturally. At school he was best at those subjects which involved his hands, and even when he played football he always went into goal. However, he never let himself become complacent and for some period of every day he would go into the yard, or the entry behind, and practise. Sometimes the younger kids would come and watch, and then he would really turn it on, trying out even more dramatic twirls and spins that he was not yet ready to perform in public. There was no movement or inch of the mace that he did not feel safe with, in the security of intimacy. But above all he practised the throw. He practised the throw, not only because it was the most difficult thing to do, but because it was the most important. All drum majors understood that. Technically it was very difficult. To throw a mace high into the air and catch it cleanly required precision of timing and reflex. There could be no second chance and no disguising failure. A player might play a wrong note and have it swallowed up by the sound of those around him, but the drum major stood out on his own. There were, too, so many things that could go wrong – strong sunlight, a gust of wind, reflexes dulled by fatigue – all could conspire to produce disaster. And yet it was the very risk involved that made the throw so important. It was an assertion of confidence and a gesture of triumph for all the world to see. The crowd loved it. When the mace went spinning into the air it would pull a roar from their throats, and an even greater roar when it was safely caught.

A week earlier, with the arrogance of youth, he had secretly thought of himself as the best catcher in the city. Now, for reasons he did not understand, his confidence had been replaced by panic and dread. The thought of the throw terrified him. Perhaps it was the setting, perhaps the possibility of failure and disgrace in front of so many people. Whatever the cause, he felt its effects eating away at his heart. Now, tossing and turning in the bed, each thought whispered to him of disaster and each minute trapped him in its boundless horizons. An eternity later, he wore himself out, and into the wake of his weariness slipped a shallow ripple of sleep. As he drifted deeper, the last sounds he was aware of were the singing voices of a couple of drunks rolling up some distant street, and in his ears their discordant voices sounded vaguely sweet.

But sleep brought no relief because he dreamed of the great day, and in his sleep he could not catch the mace. Terrible things happened. He tossed it high into the air, high as the CN Tower, and it did not come down. The whole procession piled up behind him as he stood with his arms outstretched, staring up into space. The crowd grew impatient. He begged them to wait but though he narrowed his eyes and stared into the fierce blue sky, he could find no trace of the mace. It had disappeared. And another time, just as the crowd was at its deepest, he spun it up and watched it with the eye of a hawk, but when he held up his hands to catch it, they were heavy and useless. It was as if he was wearing boxing gloves. The mace clattered to the ground and everyone laughed and shouted. Then in his dream the procession moved on and he found himself suddenly embroiled in the very heart of the battle itself. Things were going badly for King William. His soldiers couldn't get across the river and King James's men were inflicting heavy casualties. It was the crisis point of the battle. Suddenly, King William turned to him and told him to go forward and throw his mace. They tried to protect him with armour but it was too heavy and he threw it aside. Both armies were lined up along opposite banks of the river. The Catholic forces jeered when they saw him coming forward and someone shouted that they should not send a boy to do a man's job. He closed his ears to the tumult and thought only of catching the mace for his King. He threw it high, so high that every soldier in the battle could see it.

But he would never know the outcome of that throw, because he awoke with a start while the mace was still high in the air, and he was glad because he was certain that he had been going to drop it. It struck him that in one second of panic and clumsiness he could have changed the course of history for ever. Then, when he realised where he was, he lay back on the bed and felt foolish. He looked at his watch and saw that it was only five o'clock. He dozed for an hour and then decided to get up. Putting on the same clothes he had been wearing the night before he went quietly downstairs. He could hear his uncle snoring steadily.

The front room was filled with the stale smell of cigarette smoke, and an empty beer bottle that had rolled behind the settee had escaped the hurried clear-up. His uniform was laid out over a chair and he stopped to admire it. It looked immaculate, the creases razor-sharp and every silver button giving back his gleaming reflection. His mother had done a great job. After leaving the empty bottle in the kitchen, he opened the back door. The weather was clear and still, without a sign of even the slightest breeze. He felt some of his old confidence returning and he became annoyed with himself for getting worked up into such a state. Everything had gone well for him so far, and today would be no different. He started to make himself breakfast but realised he was not hungry. Anyway, it would be better to eat closer to the time when he had to leave. If he ate now, he would get hungry again later in the morning.

Closing the back door, he went quietly out, intending to go for a short walk. It was prompted by curiosity really, because he had never seen the street at such an early hour. As he walked down the entry, he heard a familiar sound and looked up to see an army helicopter shuttling across the city. Their vigilance increased his feeling of assurance. At the end of the entry he turned and walked to the top of his street. It still seemed deeply asleep. Above it towered the shipyard gantries, and above them again, the huge Goliath cranes. It was there in the yard that he had hoped to find a job when he left school, but that prospect seemed increasingly unlikely. His father had already been placed on short-time working and there were constant rumours about eventual closure. The unspoken knowledge that he would not be able to find a job when he left school had made him think about emigrating to Canada, but in his heart he didn't really want to leave, and he knew anyway that in the absence of skills or qualifications there was little chance of being accepted. Somehow his imagination was unable to grasp the possibility of there being no shipyard. It had always been there, surely it always would.

A milk float trundled round the corner. The milkman was doing his round early so that he would be able to march. He only knew the milkman by sight but as he watched him deliver his milk he felt a vague sense of brotherhood. For a second he thought of offering to help him but dismissed the idea as stupid. He retraced his steps and on his return to the house began to get ready. He had breakfast before he put on his uniform, in order to avoid the possibility of an accident. He was not yet finished when his mother came down in her dressing gown. She ran her hand over his uniform and picked off invisible specks of fluff. Everything was perfect.

Before it was time for him to leave, the whole household had come down. He had hoped to avoid his uncle and aunt. They made a great fuss over him, and his uncle looked at him through his cine-camera as if he was a film producer. He talked about how everyone in Toronto would enjoy seeing his film of 'The Twelfth'. His aunt told him yet again that they were leaving early to get a good vantage point at the junction of Ormeau Avenue and Bedford Street, and reminded him to give his 'thing' a good throw. It irritated him to hear it referred to as this, but he forced a smile and promised that he wouldn't forget. As if he could. The television cameras were always positioned at that particular spot, and it was there that he must make his big throw.

When he met up with his band at the local Orange Hall, it was obvious that everyone had made a special effort with their uniform. These were a few years old now, but no one could have guessed, and every flute and badge sparkled in the morning light. He still felt good and a few warm-up exercises served to increase his confidence. Mr Morrison came over and gave him some words of encouragement, advising him to get into the swing of things before he tried anything too fancy. A few hip-flasks were in evidence, but no one offered him anything and he would not have taken it even if they had. On the most important day of his life he needed a clear head and a steady hand.

When the east Belfast contingents had gathered, they marched across town to Carlisle Circus, the main assembly point for the procession. Spirits were high and there was much good humour, but the playing and marching were relaxed, almost as if no one wanted to risk burning themselves out. They made an exception when they passed Seaforde Street in the Short Strand. The screens were up already and soldiers stood on the corners. Without needing a command, the drummers let rip and the band played their flutes until it seemed their lungs would burst. The music swelled up and pounded like the punch of a mighty fist. The soldiers looked on bemused.

At the assembly point the road was a sea of orange sashes and band uniforms. This part of the town was strange to him, but he felt a great sense of safety among so many. Marshals directed the lodges to their correct marching positions and when they had taken this up all that was left for him to do was wait and watch. He saw bands with real drum majors whose bearing and uniform made him feel shabby and insignificant. They had heavy ornamental maces which were never thrown but which were carried with great dignity. These were mostly ex-soldiers and they marched with military precision. A breeze was blowing now and he soaked in the colours of the great fluttering banners. They were so beautiful. On them were depicted scenes from history and portraits of Protestant martyrs. Unless he read the inscriptions, he did not know what was being portrayed, but they were dramatic and powerful, and their beauty moved his heart. When he saw scenes of Protestants being burned or tied to stakes on the shore and left to drown, his soul burned with righteous anger. He would do his very best that day, not for himself, but for the people that looked down at him from these banners. Then he saw the colour party. In it were the Grand Master and Orange dignitaries. They were flanked by men carrying swords and never in his life had he seen men with such dignity and bearing. He felt privileged to walk behind them. He knew that such men would never let their people down.

After the signal was given for the colour party to set off, it took a long time before the lodge in front of the band started to move. He almost felt worried that the colour party would be at the destination before his section had even moved off. Gradually, he found himself marching down Clifton Street, the way ahead full of bands and marchers, their banners tightening in the breeze. The air reverberated with music and marching feet and he felt a small part of a great wave rolling forward, united in power and purpose. As they snaked through the main streets of the city his feet began to dance. More and more people lined the pavements and the noise and excitement seemed to increase with every step he took. Behind him the band played familiar tunes with new vigour and the drummers drummed as if their arms were made of elastic. And in front of him the great procession rolled on and forward as if nothing could stand in its way.

Halfway along Royal Avenue he tried his first throw. He had put it off as long as possible, but now he felt he had to respond to the great surge of the band he was leading. He could no longer deny their unspoken prompting. Taking a deep breath, he stepped forward into the little space that was available to him. Steadying the mace with his left hand he balanced its tip in the palm of his right hand. Then he flung it high into the air, his feet leaving the ground and his back arching tightly. The crowd cheered, but he was oblivious to everything except the spinning mace. Another roar. He had caught it. His palms were wet with sweat and he rubbed them quickly on the sides of his trousers. A terrible sickness crept into his stomach for he alone knew that he had nearly dropped it. In his eagerness he had snatched too early and the mace had clipped the top of his index finger. He knew without looking that the nail was cracked and a bruise was beginning to form. All his self-confidence began to drain away. His feet no longer danced so lightly and the music no longer carried the tune of victory. It was going to be like his worst dreams and he felt crippled with fear.

By now they were passing the City Hall and the crowds were at their deepest. His mind played desperately with possible means of escape, but each was as futile as the last. He thought of feigning illness or a sprained wrist, but he knew he could not carry it off, and he could not bear to meet the scorn that he knew he would see on the faces that looked down at him from the banners. No matter in what direction his mind raced, he knew there was to be no escape from his fate. As the procession moved on into Bedford Street, he saw it converge on him with all the crushing force of inevitability.

Suddenly the parade stopped. It did this from time to time as hold-ups worked themselves out through the length of the parade. Everyone took the chance to rest and he tried to quell his rising panic. Mr Morrison came up to him and told him he was doing fine, but just to relax a little bit and try to loosen up. He hadn't been aware that his nervousness was so obvious. With the realisation came a little feeling of shame.

The procession moved off again. At the corner of Ormeau Avenue he could see the television gantry. Across from it he saw his uncle with the cine-camera raised to his eye. He picked him out easily because he was wearing a white wind jacket and he knew his aunt and parents must be close by. Despite the fact that every fibre of his being begged for the moment to pass, he knew that the time had finally come. Each step he took now echoed slowly in his head and all around him the music seemed to reach a crescendo. Drums pounded in his ears and the brightness of the ornamental swords dazzled his eyes. The world swirled about him in a drunken confusion of burning colours and pulsing sounds. He stood at the very heart of the glorious procession and every pounding beat drew him closer to his moment. The faces of his relations became clearer and he saw the anticipation in their eyes. The crowd surged round on all sides and formed a channel through which he was to walk and the whole world was looking at him only.

He dried the little pools of moisture that were forming in his palms and held his head steady and high. Then, without thought or calculation, he threw it. He threw it higher than he had ever thrown it before. It seemed to knock at the door of Heaven itself and when it dropped it fell as if it was alive, turning and spinning like a great snake, defying anyone to capture it. He did not blink and he did not think, and his entire body reverted to pure instinct. His hand raised itself above his head and his fingers splayed open, finger-printing the air. The crowd was silent, holding its breath in a collective expectancy of failure. The snake twisted finally as if in its death dance and hurtled blindly towards the earth. His heart beat sounded louder than the loudest drum and every inch of his body tensed and felt the course of life run through it. The world turned, and turned again, and then suddenly in his right hand he felt the mace clasped cleanly and perfectly, and in his ears he heard the clamour of the crowd as cheers rose from their throats like a flock of doves released to open sky. He closed his eyes and felt the mace nestle snugly in his hand like the small hand of a loved one.

It had been a perfect catch. When he opened his eyes again, the first thing he saw was King William on a banner that had been drawn tight by the breeze. He was on his great white horse, regal and majestic, his drawn sword pointing the way ahead. As if he was calling to him, and beckoning him forward, beckoning him across the river. Across to victory.

ANGEL

THE TOO-BRITTLE toast fragmented beneath the butter knife and splintered on the plate like a jagged jigsaw puzzle. Uneaten crusts curled toothless smiles at him across the empty table, strewn with the remains of family breakfast, while the radio roared out a babble of voices, and a discordant beat hammered in his head. He buttered the pieces of toast and ate them one by one, crunching them noisily, and sipped the coffee that had lost its first heat. His head felt heavy and dull, as if he hadn't fully woken up, and each sip of coffee tasted more bitter than the last. Although he was already late, he could not bring himself to rush. He would blame the traffic. His tongue felt furred and thick, and he knew only one thing would clear it, but that was still a long way off. Staring at the cornflakes that floated in the bowl opposite him, he wondered why she never quite managed to finish anything. As his daughter grew older, it seemed that the house was constantly filled with the sound of music. Pop blared from morning to night – but he supposed it was harmless enough. There were parents with worse problems to worry about than that. She was growing up so quickly – he didn't know where the years had gone. One moment she was a child, her bedroom wall decorated with Walt Disney characters, and the next almost a teenager, her bedroom plastered with pictures of pop stars he had never heard of. Next year she would start secondary school, and some part of him regretted it very much, as if it marked the end of a childhood period that he was unwilling fully to let go. Already she was growing in complexity and self-reliance, and it hurt him a little to find her less dependent on him, pushed aside in favour of other centres in her life. He wondered where she was now – probably searching

63

for some misplaced book or pen. She had inherited his careless-
ness. The coffee was bitter to the taste and he put it down, the cup
and saucer clinking a note of sour finality.

'Is there anything else you want, Tom? I'm taking Paula to
school now.'

He shook his head and stood up from the table as if he, too, was
on the point of leaving.

'You'll not forget, now.' She lowered her voice to a whisper.
'Call at Johnstone's and say the bike has to be delivered tomorrow afternoon – it's the only time we can get it into the garage
without her being around to see it. And Tom, please don't forget
about tonight – you know it's important to her.'

'Give me a break, Claire. Of course I won't forget!'

He saw that his wife was about to respond, but she let it pass,
and he knew that she had been about to cast up past failures. He
felt aggrieved by the eternal unremitting sharpness of her
memory, but had neither the energy nor the desire to start a
slanging match. Taking his cup to the sink and rinsing it, he
plumped for reassurance.

'I promise I won't forget. When my girl steps up to sing, I'll be
standing in the front row. And I won't forget about the bike
either. Santa Claus never forgets.'

His attempt at humour evoked a silence, broken only by their
daughter clattering into the room. She was buckling her schoolbag and trailed a woollen scarf behind her like the tail of a kite.
She took up where her mother had left off.

'You'll definitely be there, won't you, Dad? You know what
time it starts – after the fireworks, right in front of the City Hall.
Right beside the Christmas tree.'

He took the trailing scarf and wrapped it snugly around her
neck.

'Don't you worry about it, Angel. Your dad'll be there all right
to hear you sing – wild horses couldn't keep me away. Do you
know your words all right?'

'Of course I do – have you not heard me singing it all week? I
only have to sing one verse by myself.'

'Don't be nervous, pet – just step right up and do your best.'

But he could see she wasn't listening to his advice, and he rummaged in the pockets of his suit to find some money to give her, but found only some keys and a book of ballot tickets. Her mother called her from the hall and she paused just long enough to give him a perfunctory peck on the cheek and tell him that she would look out for him, and when she said it he knew that it was her final reminder. With a slight flinch he realised that she was treating him as if he was the child, but he did not let it show, and, waving her goodbye, he shouted after the disappearing figure.

'Don't you worry about a thing, Angel. Your old man'll be there to see you break their hearts.'

The front door slammed shut. Immediately, he switched off the radio and soaked softly in the silence. He felt vaguely hurt. A glance at his watch told him that he was already late, but he could not bring himself to hurry. He had reached a period in life when timekeeping no longer seemed important – there was no one to impress any more, and he felt safe in the knowledge that the wheels would turn reliably without his presence. He would blame the traffic, or, better still, he would say he had stopped off to view some property. What did it matter? The house seemed strangely quiet, as if the sound had been switched off, and in the silence he searched for some interest or enthusiasm to spark the hours that lay ahead. But he found nothing, only a dreary list of petty duties and formalities that froze the day ahead with a deadening predictability and left him scrambling for some escape from its icy clutches. With growing self-pity, he imagined how crowded the city centre would be, and the difficulty involved in finding a parking space. Perhaps he could phone Johnstone's from the office – no, you could never trust some anonymous jobster at the end of a phone to do anything he promised. It would need a personal visit to evoke a cast-iron guarantee of delivery at the correct time, and even then he wouldn't believe it until he saw the damned thing safely secreted in the garage. He supposed it would be worth it when he saw the look of pleasure on her face, and watched her wobble off down the driveway on her first spin. He remembered the Christmas when he, too, had woken to find a bicycle sitting in the hall – it hadn't been brand new but his father's paint job had left it sparkling and virginally fresh. When he had opened the little packages that sat under the tree, he discovered the loudest bell in the world, a black stream-lined pump, and a narrow leather pouch that clipped on to the back of the saddle and contained an assortment of spanners and bicycle tools. The memory carried him into the past on a current of unaccustomed nostalgia, and he drifted pleasurably back to a tiny box room with a sloping ceiling, awash with selection boxes, *Topical Times* football books, torches, model planes, knitted gloves and scarves. The memories ignited a little spark of warmth in him, and he tried desperately to fan them into some kind of sustaining flame before they slipped once again into the oblivion of the past.

Perhaps Christmas wouldn't be so bad, after all it was really for the children and Paula was already bubbling with excited antici-pation. That was his pleasure now – sharing in his child's excitement and reliving, through her, the sense of wonder that the moment brought. He would go to Johnstone's first thing and get everything sorted out. But his resolution weakened as his mind returned to his wife's admonitions, and his feeling of annoyance burgeoned and blotted out all other thoughts. He grasped hold of nothing except the cold reality of it all. Christmas. What did it really mean? Families locked together with no avenues of escape, bound tightly by the hoops of some false festivity until they grew irritable and discordant; exuberant and extravagant expense that hung round the neck of the New Year; betting on the blind in the weekly poker school; kissing the young tease of a typist you'd lusted after during the previous twelve months. Drinking too much. That was something he needed no excuse for, but at least it was a chance to really push the boat out. There was no harm in it. It kept him sane, stopped him cracking under the pressure of competitive business, and, for a while at least, made him feel good inside. A few drinks, that was all, just enough to light the slow fire that made him feel warm and relaxed; a few drinks to free him from the daily burden of responsibility that grew loathsome and unending. Better, too, than anything else, it came closest to recapturing that feeling a young man has when it's the weekend, and he's a few quid in his pocket to burn, and the lads are rarin' to hit the town. It opened up the stultifying prison of the present, freed it from the restrictions of duty and routine, and invested the moment with a glow of mellow optimism. Claire didn't under-stand – she never had, always seeing it as some kind of personal rival that she had to battle and defeat, instead of something that held him together, keeping him there for her.

He let his gaze wander round the expensive kitchen and into the hall and felt angered by her apparent lack of gratitude for the material benefits his career had brought them. She was a typical woman – nagged for things until she got them, proceeded to take them for granted, and then in a remarkably short period of time, wanted something else. She was quick enough to criticise him and harp on about things as if he was the worst in the world, but she wasn't so quick to appreciate the hard graft that had gone into getting them where they were today. As if he would forget! Who did she think he was? Didn't he dote on his daughter? Didn't he worship the very ground she walked on? She'd no right to snipe at him like that when she knew he would cut his hand off before he'd hurt the child.

His anger galvanised him into energy, and, gathering up his coat and briefcase, he hurried out to the car. He turned on the radio to catch the news. A man shot dead in front of his wife and child . . . a litany of internecine political squabbles . . . industrial initiatives . . . snow falling on the Glenshane Pass. It washed over him without registering and he switched it off again. The roads were slow and congested, and he noted the number of traffic police about. He would have to be careful – the days were long gone when a nod in the right quarter would smooth over a charge.

The office was busy and he sought to cloak his lateness with a purposeful display of unloading a sheaf of paperwork from his briefcase. His secretary informed him that there had been no calls, and no one had been looking for him. He opened his post while watching a junior typist balance precariously on a desk as she tried to put up Christmas decorations, joking with her about falling and possible insurance claims, and offering to hold her ankles, until the girl coloured and climbed down with the job unfinished. Slowly and with some difficulty, he clambered on to the desk and fastened the line of tinsel. The sudden movement had reminded him that he wasn't feeling good, and as he sat down, the incessant thunder of typewriters rattled his brain.

The morning dragged by and he continued the pretence of being busy without actually ever completing anything of import-ance. He shuffled papers round his desk and made some phone calls, but nothing could distract him from the knowledge that he needed a drink. He tried to postpone it as long as possible and had another coffee, but it didn't help. The clock seemed to have stopped. Eventually, as lunch approached, his impatience and restlessness overcame him, and collecting some keys from the office safe, he told his secretary that he was going to value some commercial properties. When she asked him where he could be reached, he replied that he would be on the move and would phone back at intervals, then he put on his coat and set off into the city streets. He pulled the collar of the coat up round his neck and dug his hands deep into his pockets. It was cold enough for snow. A bloody white Christmas – that was the last thing he needed; all right for the front of Christmas cards, but misery for everyone else. His dismal thoughts were interrupted by a slap on his back.

'Sell us a house, mister. Any oul hovel'll do.'

It was George Monroe, a fellow traveller of old, an accomplice in crime. They were glad they had found each other – company made each feel less swamped by the overwhelming mass of anonymous faces that flowed about them.

'In search of a little respite, Tom? Do you want a companion? I owe it to your wife to keep an eye on you!'

Their journey to Mooney's was lengthened by the density of the crowd, and at times it was easier to flow temporarily with it into divergent channels than attempt to fight against its powerful tide. Every other person seemed about to collapse under a burden of parcels, and the polythene bags they carried, emblazoned with trade names, flapped like flags in the sharp-toothed wind. A Salvation Army band played in the pedestrian precinct, and his eye caught a glimpse of young girls in dark uniforms and bonnets, quivering the air with a parabola of ribboned tambourines.

Queues were forming to enter the big stores and in each doorway collecting tins were rattled for silver. Buskers competed with piped carols, and an old man without a coat sold rolls of cheap wrapping paper. A troupe of orange-robed Hari Krishnas wove their tinkling, chanting way through the crowds, while an old man, armoured in a breastplate of scripture, distributed tracts. A few yards further on, they fluttered to the pavement and mingled underfoot with bills advertising seasonal offers in the wine store. A mother cut across their path, trailing behind her a screaming child, and at every step the crowd seemed deeper and more desperate.

'Hell, Tom, the whole world's gone crazy!'

'If we get to Mooney's we'll deserve a medal as well as a drink.'

They pushed on, steering each other in the best direction by little tugs and pulls of their coats, pausing at intervals to ponder the best route, until eventually they reached the entrance to the bar. A squeal of young girls breezed out through the doors, clutching at collars and coats in anticipation of the biting cold, and giving a second's preview of the crowded inside, long enough to show that they had found no refuge of tranquillity or seclusion. As they shouldered their way through the mêlée inside, his companion turned and grimaced.

'There's no room in the inn – it's standing room only.'

'Let's go to Henry's, George – this'd put your head away. There's not room to raise your elbow.'

Reluctantly, both men turned and edged their way back out on to the street, then trudged somewhat miserably round the corner to the less fashionable Henry's. At a corner table, they found spare seats and, squeezing into them, opened their coats with simultaneous sighs of relief. A round of drinks was set up and savoured. For him, the first was always the sweetest and the only one he ever really tasted. It felt good, and he settled back into the chair.

'Thank God, George, Christmas only comes once a year. You'd need to go into training to survive it. It's getting worse every year.'

'It'd be all right, Tom, if it didn't end up costing you an arm and a leg. Marion writes cheques like there's no tomorrow, buys expensive presents for half the world – excluding me, of course – but what really kills me is what she spends on that witch of a mother, and what I get in return. The old bat's loaded up to the eyeballs, and when she gives you a present it's something like a set of coathangers, or some plastic knick-knack that she bought in the 50p shop.'

'I can't complain about Claire – she's not bad really, keeps things within reason. It still costs, mind you – I suppose there's no way round it. Listen, McClenaghan told me this joke about mothers-in-law. "My mother-in-law visits us every Christmas. Next year we're going to let her in."'

The two men leaned forward over the table and chuckled expansively. Monroe took out two cigars from an inside pocket and they lit up.

'Sometimes, George, I think it'd be really good to go away over Christmas. Go to the sun, or even skiing. Don't suppose, though, Claire'd ever agree – she's a bit of a traditionalist.'

'Now you're talking. I've always fancied the idea myself. I bumped into Perry Foster last week, and he's off to some Austrian ski resort.'

'Perry Foster? I can't imagine him on skis, shooting down some mountain.'

'Neither can he, Tom. Never puts his feet anywhere other than under the bar. Après-ski all day long. And, I'll tell you better still – he doesn't go alone. Takes a bit of fluff with him.'

'The old dog,' laughed Tom. 'How does he get away with it?'

'The wife goes her own way. No questions asked, no lies told. Perfect relationship.'

The two men supped their drinks, and blew smoke while they reflected on the escapee and their minds conjured up images of snow-covered chalets, blazing log fires, and easy company.

'Good luck to him, George, and all, but there has to be something said for a family Christmas and carving the old turkey.'

'True enough, true enough.'

There was a pause in the conversation as both men tried to

convince themselves that they didn't envy Foster's bid for freedom.

'A bad business that, last night, Tom. You'd think they'd give it a break for a couple of weeks – call a truce or something, out of respect for the time of year.'

'Those boys have respect for nothing.'

'That's the truth. Did it right in front of his wife and child. Some Christmas that kid's going to have – now and for the rest of her life.'

'Paula's class is doing the carols tonight at the City Hall. She's singing a verse on her own. I'm going to hear her. You should come, George – hear a real performer.'

'Like to, Tom, but it's my night on duty at the golf club. Anyway, between late night shopping and fireworks, the town'll be hell. There'll not be breathing space.'

Their conversation was temporarily halted by the approach of a mutual friend.

'You two boys are starting early today. Am I the only one working?'

The newcomer smiled down at the two drinkers and placed a hand on each of their shoulders.

'Sit down, Ross, and take the weight off your feet. And you're not doing much work yourself, standing in here. Has the Law Society started allowing you boys to go out touting for clients? Tom and I are just having a wee jar while we sort out the world's problems. What can I get you?'

'A hot whiskey'd go down well – it's freezing out there. But just one, now – I can't stay.'

As George manoeuvred his way to the bar, the two men smiled at each other, knowingly.

'He's a desperate case. You're keeping bad company, Tom. Have you run out of houses to sell?'

'Plenty of houses, Ross, too many bloody houses. The whole world's putting their house up for sale and buying someone else's. It's like one big property roundabout that never stops.'

'If you're so busy, Tom, how can you find time to sit in here?'

'Delegation, Ross, delegation – the first skill of management.

And sure isn't it boys like me keeping the likes of you in work. The only difference is that you charge them almost double for half the work.'

'True enough, but you get to work with a better class of customer. You wouldn't want to meet some of the trash I'm rubbing shoulders with every day. Some days you feel you should disinfect yourself before you go home. Money wouldn't pay you.'

'Money never comes easily, Ross – we all have to grub in the dirt sometimes, and the richer the man, the more dirt he's grubbed in. You can bet on it. But, tell me this – what do you think of this new tax? Is it not going to hit your pocket as much as ours?'

'There's ways and means. A bit of artistic accountancy goes a long, long way. Our accountant's the most creative man I know. But here we go.'

The drinks arrived, and they settled back into the mellow depths of the afternoon, rounds of drinks and conversation easing them through the hours. They went out for food and returned, then, for a change of scenery, made the short journey to Mooney's. Familiar faces came and went and the hours passed, gliding along on well-oiled rails, journeying through business talk, gossip, reminiscences, solemn bouts of setting the world right, and always the clink of glasses and the palliative company of old friends. He felt safe and sheltered from the madness outside, and gradually the day lost its boundaries of time.

The coldness of the air made him flinch, and for a moment he felt tempted to return to the warm security behind him, rather than embark on the hazardous and uncertain journey that duty told him stretched ahead, but the warm glow inside him mingled with the memory of his promise to his daughter and compelled him into the undiminished flux. He felt strangely at one with the anonymous faces that flowed around him, and he nodded and smiled, as if to old friends. He bumped into someone and apologised with a bestowal of the season's greetings and an elaborate bow. His step took on the jaunty spring of a man cresting the waves and, for the first time, he began to feel finely festive in mood. He found himself singing along with a carol that blared from an outside speaker, and his right hand conducted imaginary choirs. Confronted by a collecting tin, he searched in the depths of his pockets before chinking a stream of coins into it, then sported the badge on the breast of his coat like a medal of honour.

The Christmas lights were on now, and the city centre crystallised in a white brightness as lights and neon tinsel stretched across the main streets like fluorescent icing on a cake. For a second, the noise and lights confused and disorientated him – he had drunk too much too quickly – but he laughed at himself and, with a little skip in his step, headed onward. As he passed a jewellery shop, he remembered that he had not yet found a Christmas present for his wife. He edged himself into a space at the window and viewed the contents, not quite managing to focus his attention exclusively on any one object. The display was a meaningless and undifferentiated grotto of trinkets and baubles that gave him no guide or inspiration. Still, finding something would remove the need for a return shopping trip and at that moment his spirit of well-being encompassed even his wife. A neck chain or bracelet would probably fit the bill, might even buy some short-lived credit. It was a good idea.

The shop was not as crowded as he had expected, and in a few moments a girl came to serve him. She wore a black suit, and a white blouse that seemed to have lost none of its crispness, and only the tiny beads of damp on her top lip spoke of a long, hard day. She smiled at him and he smiled back, his eyes drinking in her youthful freshness, and everything about her gratified his senses. She greeted him as if he was the most important customer of the day. Her glossy black hair was cut in a bob and flowed with the movement of her head, accentuating the whiteness of her skin and the soft red mouth. He wondered what she would be like. He looked at her, slowly savouring each part of her as he had savoured that first drink. She was young, but she wasn't a child. Looking over her shoulder he caught his reflection in a mirror – he wasn't over the hill yet, there were still plenty of good years left. He wondered if he could still cut it. Leave aside a couple of meaningless indiscretions along the way, and, by and large, he had been a faithful husband, and what was his reward? A dried-up husk of a relationship that functioned in a mechanical way, stuttering along with predictable, timetabled pretences of passion. His eyes rested on her neck as she leaned across the counter to show him a series of gold chains. He wanted to touch her. If he no longer had youth, he did possess the maturity money brought, and he had read that some girls found that an attractive feature. He teased her gently, and when she mentioned prices, he dismissed the subject with a 'sure it's only money'. She smiled at his jokes, but he couldn't detect any personal edge to her professional charm. He bought a gold neck chain and was vaguely aware of spending more money than he had intended. She wrapped it carefully, making a decorative package topped with a pink bow, and for a second he thought of saying that the present was for her, but it wasn't like buying a barmaid a drink, and as he watched the manicured fingernails tie the bow, a little seed of doubt was sown in his optimism. She probably had a trail of followers after her . . . she wouldn't be interested in the likes of him . . . he was old enough to be her father. But, a decade earlier, then it would have been a different story. He consoled himself with this belief as he left the shop. A gold necklace and a bottle of her favourite perfume – that would do the job. There couldn't be any complaints about that, no unspoken suggestions of negligence. In the outside window, his eyes fixed on a digital clock and with some shock it struck him that he had lost track of the time. He would have to hurry if he was to get a good position for the carols. He wondered if Paula was nervous before her big moment, but he knew with pride that she would be able to carry it off. She had always been like that – a real trouper – and he was proud of her.

As he stepped out into the street, there was a sudden explosion, and the night air shattered with splinters of light. Involuntarily, he stepped back into the shelter of the shop doorway, startled and a little frightened, and then, as a garland of light twisted in the sky, he realised with a feeling of foolishness that the firework display had already begun. He would have to hurry. Following the momentary frieze of frozen stars, he walked as quickly as his co-ordination would let him, and threaded his way uneasily through the milling crowds. Fiery rockets screeched into the night sky above him and fragmented into a fall of luminous petals, while fluorescent reds and yellows ignited the dark pockets of the night and cascaded into nothingness. Spangled rosettes of blossom burst into transient life and were greeted by applause and gasps of pleasure. He hurried on. The bicycle – he had forgotten the bloody bicycle. He stopped and looked at his watch, but knew he would never make it in time. First thing in the morning he would phone; better still, he would go round himself and sort the whole thing out. A bright tracery of light laced the sky ahead, and as he set off again, a final crescendo and eruption of colours showering over the green domes of the City Hall signalled the end of the display.

He could see the covered stage at the side of the giant Christmas tree and he could hear the children's voices rising up in song. His tired eyes fixed on the bright star, and he left the pavement for the greater freedom of the road. The sound of 'O little town of Bethlehem' called him on, and he knew nothing could prevent him from reaching his destination. He was a good father – no one could deny him that, and he knew Paula would be looking for him, wanting him to be there. He would never let her down. He felt warm inside, benevolent to all men and at peace with the world. It was a special time – he couldn't deny the emotions and feelings bubbling up inside him. All the cynicism and world-weariness washed away, and he opened his heart to the holiness of the hour. He thought of all the mothers who, at that moment, were wrapping presents for their children and sealing them with love; of fathers working overtime to gather up the means of providing their families with the festive feast; of the children with every sense alive and tingling. In his imagination, he saw the great snow plough clearing the Glenshane Pass, throwing the fresh, white snow to the sides of the road, its yellow lights splitting the dark and lighting the way for travellers. He caught some of the words of the carol, and he thought, too, of the city he loved, tinselled and shimmering in the safety of the fire that burned so brightly and fended off the wolves, who waited and watched in the darkness of the woods.

He was almost there now. He was conscious of bumping into people, and aware that people were looking at him, but nothing mattered, he had to be there to hear his Angel. Shouldering his way through the spectators, he reached a position against the crash barriers in front of the nativity scene. He could see her now, and his hands gripped the cold metal bar. She was dressed in white, with a silver tinfoil halo hovering above her head and cardboard wings fluttering precariously in the breeze. Yellow light bathed the crib and lit the children's intense faces as they grouped round the manger and the holy infant. He wanted to call out to her, let her know he was there, but the terrible sanctity of the scene bound him in silence. He wanted to kneel, but the press behind him prevented any change in his position. The voices of the children rose on fragile wings through the cold night air, heralding the miraculous birth. He too wanted to worship, bring his gifts, and as their music faded into the darkness, tears of remorse started to his eyes.

SEARCHING THE SHADOWS

FATHER DONNELLY would sort it out – they would listen to him. It was all some kind of mistake, and if anyone could sort it out the Father could. He had always been good to the boy, and since her husband's death had taken a special interest in him. Yes, he was always asking her about how Anthony was getting on. Any time he saw her he never failed to ask. Even though he must have had a thousand other things to worry about, he never once forgot to ask how the boy was doing. Father Donnelly was a good priest all right, and she'd never hear anyone say a bad word about him – if the church had a few more like him, perhaps the pews would be fuller. All through John's illness he had been very faithful and had been there at the bedside at the very end. Thanks be to God, the end had been peaceful – after all the weeks of turmoil and pain he had just slipped away, and the Father's presence had made it all so much easier, so much more dignified.

She went into the kitchen and boiled up the kettle for the third time. She expected them both back at any minute, and a cup of tea would be the thing that was needed. She wondered what was keeping them. Taking a teacloth, she wiped the cups and saucers, then searched in the cupboard for the china milk jug which was reserved for special visitors. The last time she had used it was on the day of the funeral.

The sound of the gate opening sent her scurrying back into the living room and to the window. Pressing her face against the net curtain, she peered into the falling gloom, but there was no one there. As she turned away, she heard a neighbouring door open and shut. She sat down and stared for a second at the silent television picture, but in her restlessness, nothing seemed to register, nothing seemed to make sense. Her eyes dropped to her hands, and she saw, to her surprise, that she was still holding the milk jug. She looked at it closely. It was part of a teaset they had been given as a wedding present. That seemed such a long time ago. There was only the jug and a few saucers left. She had always loved the pretty blue flowers frozen against the coolness of the white. She didn't know what had happened to the set – a piece broken here and a piece there, she supposed; over the years it must all have mounted up like little bits breaking off your life. Anthony could be careless at times – she had to admit that. Sometimes he was so clumsy, almost as if his hands didn't work properly. He'd never have made an altar boy, that was sure, but then not every boy was meant to be an altar boy. It wasn't his fault – it was just the way he was made and there was no changing it now. She looked at the clock. Where was Anthony? Where was Father Donnelly? It was over an hour since the Father had gone out to bring him back. Where could they be?

She took the jug back into the kitchen and placed it on the tray, moving everything a fraction of an inch like pieces on a chess board. Anthony had shouldered his father's coffin like a man that day. He had looked so well in his Sunday clothes she had felt proud of him. He had carried the day off as well as any boy could, and better than some she could think of. It was only after John's death that the real problems had started. He had always been a lively, boisterous child but as he moved through his teenage years he had grown headstrong and difficult. He wasn't a bad lad at heart – he really wasn't. She knew him better than anyone else, and she would swear on the Holy Book itself that deep down he had a good heart. Didn't he look after her like a nurse the time last winter when she had gone down with the virus, and didn't he even send her a lovely card on Mother's Day? There were too many people quick to pass judgment when they never saw the whole picture. John had known how to handle him, how to get the best out of him – when to laugh at him and when to reach for the belt. They had been the best of friends, and when they had fallen out it had never lasted for long. It was only since his father's death that Anthony had gone off the rails.

No matter how hard she tried, she couldn't get close to him or get him to talk to her in the way he had done when he was younger. Now, he just seemed to clam up, or brush her attempts aside with an indifference that he couldn't have realised was so hurtful to her. Perhaps it was because he felt he was the man of the house and no longer needed to give an account of his actions. Lord knows, there were plenty of others more than ready to give that account, and ready at the drop of a hat to put their seal of judgment on his soul. Hypocrites the lot of them! And the school was the worst – summoning her like the courts themselves to listen to a recitation of his misdemeanours and, by implication, her shortcomings as a parent. Their holier-than-thou attitude made her sick. What did they know about bringing up a boy on the little money she had to make ends meet and living where she did? There weren't too many teachers who had any idea of what life was like on the estate. At the end of school, it was into their cars and home to nice houses in the suburbs. She'd like to see them bringing up their families where she had to and see then how many found it all plain sailing. They were supposed to be the experts and if they couldn't get through to him, how was she supposed to do it? Half the time, anyway, she was sure it wasn't the boy's fault. They had labelled him from his first week in the place, and it had gone ahead of him wherever he went. 'Never produces his best' – that was what was written on his report. Well, wasn't that what they were paid for in the first place – to bring the best out of him, to develop his talents? The school was more of a failure than he was. They had no cause to throw stones at anyone. She was glad he had finished with it. Some day, though, he would show them what he was capable of, show them all that he could achieve something when he put his mind to it. She knew he had it in him, she knew that given the right opportunities and a bit of luck, he could make something of himself. He was going through a difficult spell – lots of children went through them – but he would come through to the other side. She was sure of it.

Outside in the street a dog barked an angry threat at some passing shadow. Somewhere, a car door slammed. She went back to the window and searched the dusk for a sign, but the row of identical houses opposite only stared impassively back, like indifferent eyes.

It was over an hour since the two men had called for her son and taken him away. When she had opened the front door they were standing there, one on the step and a younger man just inside the gate. At first, she had thought it was a collection, just another of the endless 'freewill' collections for some aspect of the cause that your pocket begrudged, but your fear of being marked out as soft on the struggle compelled you to give. Struggle? The very word stuck in her throat. Wasn't every day of her life a struggle to get by? Wasn't her very existence one long battle against bitter and vindictive odds? No one had any right to come to her door and talk of struggle, when it took every penny she had, and every drop of energy her body possessed just to keep her head above the waves. Every single penny she had in her purse was precious and it wasn't right that a widow should have to give from the little she had. But although these thoughts had filled her head, it was a smile on her lips which greeted the two callers, a smile which only faded when she realised that they hadn't come for money. The older man was in his forties and she didn't recognise his face. He wore a green unbuttoned jacket, a white open-necked shirt, blue jeans and tan coloured boots. Stiff tufts of red hair stuck sharply at intervals from the elasticated sides of a green tartan cap. Behind him, the younger boy seemed fresh-faced by comparison. He had blond spiked hair, and a pale face with nervous blue eyes which flitted nervously about without settling on anything for more than a few seconds. She had seen him before and as she stared at him he lowered his eyes to the ground. Then she remembered he was one of Annie Walshe's boys, but before she could put a first name to him, his companion addressed her by name.

'Mrs McCann, we'd like a wee word with Anthony, if you don't mind?'

And before she had time to reply, he had stepped past her into the house, almost gently and without brushing against her, but ignoring her protests. The blond boy followed them both and stood silently in the doorway. Without looking at him, she could feel his blue eyes flickering round the room which was her home, taking in the blue vinyl suite with its black-throated rip; the cream tiled fireplace with its dark peacock tail of smoke stains; the mantelpiece with its brass ornaments, and neat pile of unpaid bills snuggling behind the ship's wheel clock which was a wedding present from the girls with whom she used to work. She could feel his eyes violating the privacy of her home, prying into every secret corner, recording and remembering everything. She knew from the expression in her son's eyes that he was frightened, but when she asked what they wanted to talk to him about, no one spoke. She had asked again and again, holding on to her son with one arm as if she wouldn't let him go without an answer. Then the older of the two men had spoken but his face betrayed none of his thoughts.

'Anthony knows, don't you, son?'

Then her own son had pushed her arm away, pushed it almost roughly, and they were gone. She had gone to the door and watched them until they were lost in the darkness.

She had sent for Father Donnelly right away – even in her reeling confusion that had seemed the right thing to do. Desperately, she tried to keep control of herself as convulsive images of punishment beatings and kneecappings fired her mind frantic with fear. Father Donnelly had come right away – to his eternal credit he was a priest who was always there when he was needed. He had reassured her that nothing was wrong – this sort of thing happened every night of the week and there was no reason from the men's manner to think that they wanted anything other than to talk to the boy. He asked for a description of the two men and told her he would go and find out what it was all about. His calm, confident manner had helped her to regain control and the Father was right, it wasn't as if they had come bursting through the door with hurley sticks in their hands, shouting and cursing. They wanted to talk to the boy – that was what they had said and when they had done that he would come home again. They were probably on their way at that very moment. She went to the window again and peered out hopefully. A skinny, limping shiver of a dog patrolled the street, stopping only to sniff the occasional gatepost. A lad went by with two video cassettes under his arm, followed a few moments later by a man on a bicycle, and then there was no one.

She was sure he couldn't have done anything to provoke their anger. He hadn't been in any kind of trouble for a good six months. It was true there had been that squabble with Jamesy Rogan over ownership of some old bicycle wheels that had ended in a split lip and a nose bleed, but that hardly amounted to anything more than a boyish dispute with no interest for anyone other than those directly concerned. If there had been anything else she would have heard about it, but she was sure he had done nothing wrong. You didn't get your legs shot to pieces over bicycle wheels.

Then a terrible thought struck her. Perhaps they wanted him to do some job for them. Her mind shuddered as she imagined what they might use him for – carrying something from one safe house to another, acting as a look-out on some shadowy street corner or a dumb decoy to draw the heat off someone else. An hysterical welter of scenes played out in her imagination, each more nightmarish than the last, eating away a little more of her self-control, and each one closing with the same lacerating image of a bloody and mutilated corpse. And yet, even in her rising panic, her memory assured her that her worst fears were not foolish. The image of Patrick Killen's funeral vibrated like a plucked string, repeating incessantly a numbing and insistent note. She saw again the mother break away from restraining hands to fling herself on the coffin of her youngest son, and heard, too, that high-pitched scream which the winter wind seemed to carry and distort, until it sounded like the wail of a frightened and wounded animal. That terrible scream echoed now in her head, coiling its corrosive and caustic strands tightly round her senses, while other voices whispered that Patrick Killen was no more than a year older than her own son.

She plucked a cigarette from the packet hidden behind the radio – she had already smoked her daily ration, but this was an emergency. She changed the hiding place at regular intervals to stop him finding them. Soon she would run out of hiding places, and then she would have to carry them round with her everywhere she went. When that time came, she would give them up altogether.

With shaking hands, she lit the cigarette and took deep drags, holding it tightly before angling her head upwards and exhaling slowly and steadily. Still the whispering voices refused to be silent and more names were remembered, the names of other young men who had died in their teens. She remembered them all. It was a list which grew longer all the time and showed no sign of coming to an end. She had every right to be worried about her son – it would be a poor mother who wouldn't be. And God knew she had tried to be a good mother, tried her very best to provide for him and bring him up as well as she could without the help of a husband. She gave herself a modest testimonial, cataloguing her sacrifices and her faithfulness, but all the time growing feelings of guilt spoke of her inadequacies and failings. With regret she recalled their argument over his habit of taking her cigarettes. She had quarrelled with her son over a cigarette, and now he was gone, and she didn't know where he was, or what was happening to him. She could feel tears welling up in her eyes, but she held them back. It wasn't even that she begrudged him the cigarettes, but they were bad for him, and they were the single luxury she had left in her life. If only he would come home, she would never keep anything back from him again. She prayed fervently that God would give her back her son, give him into the custody of Father Donnelly, and send him safely home to his mother's arms. She made sincere promises in return and felt a flush of piety that she suddenly realised had faded from her life over the years. Maybe she would go to a retreat and re-commit her faith, re-dedicate herself to the church. If Father Donnelly brought home her boy, she would be in God's eternal debt, and it was a debt she would repay faithfully if it took her the rest of her life. Feeling calmer in her soul now that she had struck a kind of bargain, reached an understanding with God, she began to make preparations for their return.

Going into the kitchen, she took some biscuits from a tin and arranged them on a plate. She boiled the kettle again and wiped some crumbs off the kitchen table. When Anthony came home she wasn't going to let him out of her sight – it didn't matter if she had to walk round ten feet behind him, she would do anything rather than risk losing him. And if he didn't like it, well, that was just too bad. Nothing would make her endure again the miseries of these last few hours. Nothing would make her sit through this mixture of fear and uncertainty. She knew deep down he would care enough about her feelings to understand. Impatience and a growing sense that their return was imminent drew her back to the living room window. It was much darker now, and she put her pale face close to the net curtain in an attempt to see into the street. There was a musty smell from the curtain and its creases hung lifelessly and irregularly to within an inch of the window ledge where little glass animals marched across flaking paint. She moved closer still, until her motionless face wore the net like a veil, her eyes searching the shadows for some coming. It was difficult to see, difficult to tell what was real and what was imaginary, and as her hands clutched at the thin net the light played tricks with her eyes, leaving her confused and uncertain. Then, as the street lamps glowed deeper orange, she heard the sound of footsteps and without waiting a second longer she rushed to the door, her heart giving thanks and her hands brushing cigarette ash off the hem of her skirt. Her fingers fumbled with the lock and as she flung the door open, her hand slipped and the door banged loudly against the wall. The noise vibrating in her ears deafened her, until it quivered to a silence, and with it came a realisation that the steps were fading. She rushed to the open gate and peered after the shapes of three men disappearing into the distance. Her hands grasped the metal gate and its coldness burnt her with disappointment and frustration. She felt as if she was being mocked by some unseen watcher and she stifled a curse of bitterness and anger. A knot of nausea tightened in her stomach and sent her scurrying back into the house.

With trembling hands, she lit another cigarette, then cradled her head and rocked gently from side to side. Surely God was punishing her, surely she had done something terrible and this was his way of punishing her. But her punishment was too great, more than she could bear – more than anyone could be expected to bear. He had taken her husband and dealt her a heavy blow and now, did a loving God plan to take her only son and crush the last vestiges of strength out of her faltering soul? If only Father Donnelly would come she would kneel and kiss his hand, then confess every miserable, selfish sin that besmirched her soul's righteousness. Perhaps all this was God's way of testing her, of purging her in the flames of suffering to bring her back to the first flowering of faith she had known as a young woman. A torrent of ardent promises flowed from her, each more desperate than the last, each washed clean by the sincerity of fear.

She stubbed out the cigarette in the overflowing ashtray, sending a fine spray of ash into the air, then went again to the window. Her veiled eyes struggled to penetrate the shadowy world for some harbinger of hope. A car passed, briefly lighting up a square of tousled and tangled garden; in a house opposite, someone switched on a bedroom light, then pulled the curtains, giving her a fleeting glimpse of a wardrobe with a cardboard box on top of it, but the street itself seemed empty of people or any sign of life.

She was aware of the musty smell again. A sudden impulse took her to go in search of Anthony herself – anything would be better than the terrible waiting – but where would she go to look? She had no idea of where she might even start, and what if Father Donnelly and the boy returned and she wasn't there? No, she would have to wait. Keep busy, that was the best way. She poked some life into the dwindling fire and started to tidy the pile of old newspapers and magazines gathering dust in the corner. In the middle of the pile, she found the card he had sent her on Mother's Day. It had a picture of daffodils and a lovely verse. She knew she hadn't thrown it out. Holding on to it tightly, she treasured it as confirmation of the goodness that only she seemed to know was in him. She wanted to wave it in the air like a flag for all the world to see, as indisputable testimony to the goodness he carried deep in his heart. She would put the card on the mantelpiece and show it to Father Donnelly when they returned. Anthony would be embarrassed, but she had come too far to worry about things like that. Let God send her son back to her and she would take better care of him than any other mother in Derry. Let him come home safe and well, and she would pay back her debt to God with abundant interest.

With guilt, she remembered all the times in recent days when she had felt dissatisfied and weary of her life. If only she could return to those times, she would consider herself fortunate. If only she could get through her remaining days without too much pain, scrape by with the minimum of suffering, then she would think of herself as blessed. Life would no longer be conceived of in terms of happiness, or even in vague expectations of it, but purely in the absence of misery. She felt that perhaps she had found some insight into existence, some safe route which would take her through the troubled times which lay ahead. Let God allow her to go back to where she had been a few hours previously and she would never again complain or lament the lot which life had appointed to her. Wasn't it true, also, that God never apportioned a burden greater than could be borne? She would have to be strong, stronger than she had ever been, and pull her life together again, and not only for herself but also for her son. Things couldn't go on in this way. Even if he came home safely tonight, she knew there would be other times when he would bring her heartbreak.

Slowly and painfully, she forced herself to face up to the reality she had tried so hard to avoid. If she didn't do something now, something to take him in hand, then they were heading for disaster. There was no point trying to hide away from it any more. Even though she loved him as her only son she could not pretend any longer to be blind to the signs which grew more evident by the day. She forced herself to think of them, suddenly frightened that any omission would bring down a worse punishment on the boy, in the same way that a bad confession could damn the soul. Last Easter, he had stolen money out of her purse and then denied any knowledge of it. Although he had never admitted it, she knew he had taken it, just as she knew he had stolen the football from the school store. When the letter had come from the school, she had blindly and desperately supported his story that someone else had given it to him, but in her heart she knew it was a lie. If only he had told her that a miserable ball meant so much to him, enough to make him a thief, she would have found the money to buy him one. But he hadn't told her, and that was the heart of the problem. As he had grown older he had stopped talking to her in any meaningful way. With every year that passed, another area of his life was shrouded in secrecy and silence. Soon, there would be nothing shared or open between them, save the dwindling time he spent in the house, a house which he treated increasingly like a boarding house – somewhere to eat and sleep.

She paused in her thoughts to lift a few pieces of coal from the scuttle at the side of the hearth and place them in strategic positions on the smouldering fire. She used the tips of her fingers, then flicked them over each other to dispel the accumulated blackness. Taking a tissue, she wet it with spittle, then rubbed vigorously at the residue. When she had finished, she wet it again and tried to clean some of the black stains from the tiles on the breast of the fireplace, but they were too deeply ingrained, and she threw the tissue into the fire with a frustrated twist of her wrist. The house had never been a palace, but lately she had let it slip into a state of neglect. When this was all over and she had pulled together the pieces of her life, she would give the whole house a spring clean and spend a little money on fixing it up. Maybe even the welfare would be able to help her get some new furniture. She would try to make it a better home for her son, somewhere he could be proud of, somewhere he could bring his friends whenever he wanted.

She wondered who his friends were and why he never talked about them. Once, she had tried to ask about them, but he had turned her away with evasive answers and not a single name had been forthcoming. If only she could get him to talk to her – that would be the start of things getting better. If only she could find the key which would open up his sullen indifference. Did he not realise how much that hurt her? She remembered with a moment-

ary flicker of affection when he was little and used to come to her
with all his joys and troubles, how he would climb on to her knee
and snuggle into the protective warmth she offered him. He had
made her feel like a mother then, and she longed to have that same
feeling return. If only he could realise that she too had needs, and
that he was the only important thing she had left, he might come
back to her and give her the affection which would help her
survive in an indifferent world.

But there were, too, other sins to be confessed, and it would be
a dangerous thing to try to hide any of them from God, who
already knew them all. Anthony had stolen tools from the
workmen's hut when the community centre was being built, and
he had been involved in the vandalism at the primary school. And
that was not all. She confessed them all, keeping back nothing that
she knew to be true. There were many things which she did not
know about, things which happened without her knowledge and
which she had no way of discovering. Perhaps she was grateful
that it was so.

When she had finished, a feeling of cleansing washed over her.
It was as if the slate had been wiped clean, and she had laid the
foundations for a fresh start. Sown the seed of a new beginning.
Now that this had been done, she felt entitled to think positively
about the coming days and even to plan their life together, setting
moments in the future like small stones across a stream. Her eyes
caught the jug on the table. She had always loved its smooth
coolness and the blue flowers in the pattern. It was a pity there
were so few pieces left. She wondered if it would be possible to
find a shop which still sold that particular set. It reminded her of
her wedding day. Perhaps she should have looked after the set
more carefully – there were so few things surrounding her which
brought back good memories. She straightened some creases on
the tablecloth and moved one of the saucers to cover a stain she
had never noticed before. It was such a cold night that Father
Donnelly would need a good warm cup of tea to put some heat
into him. She remembered with anger that they hadn't even given
Anthony time to put a coat on. Who did they think they were,
dragging a boy out of his own home without so much as an

apology or a word of explanation – who gave them the right to barge into someone's home and act like policemen? Sure, weren't they worse than any policeman ever was? It would be the last time she put her hand in her pocket for a collection – she didn't care what anybody said, she'd had her fill. They had taken enough out of her heart this night to pay off any debt they thought she owed. Let any of them come to her house ever again and she would show them the door.

Her anger carried her back to the window where the curtain veiled her face once more. It was so difficult to see anything with certainty. The light played tricks on her eyes as she searched the heavy dusk which had fallen everywhere and coated the world with a smothering film of greyness, leaving the streets vague and undefined.

Then, suddenly, her hopes clutched frantically at a dark figure who had appeared as if by magic through a wall of greyness, and who was hurrying towards her from the distance. There was something immediately familiar about his busy, scurrying motion and his broad-shouldered outline. She was sure it was him, and surer by the second, as that scampering, scurrying gait carried him closer to her door. Her eyes strained eagerly to see past his broad form and searched desperately for her son, but she could not see him.

Rushing away from the window towards the door, she tried to convince herself that he would be there when she opened it, standing on the doorstep safe and well, with Father Donnelly's protective arm around him.

As her fingers fiddled clumsily with the lock, she told herself that if only she believed with enough faith, it would be true. Then, flinging open the door, she stared past the Father's looming form which almost filled the doorway, hoping beyond hope that her son would step into the light from the priest's shadowy wake. With fear in her heart, she looked for the first time into the eyes of the priest, and knew before he spoke that he had returned without her son. She gave a whimper of despair, and for a second she thought that she was going to faint, but he stretched out his arms and supported her back into the living room, murmuring assurances that she no longer believed. The priest's face was flushed and his grey hair was dishevelled; all the time he was telling her that everything was going to be fine, and all the time she knew he was lying.

Regaining some control, she confronted him with a voice which demanded the truth.

'Where's Anthony, Father? Where's my son?'

'He's all right, Eilish, he's all right. I've seen him not twenty minutes ago, and he's all right. Believe me, Eilish, they haven't harmed the boy in any way.'

'But where is he? Why didn't he come back with you? If he's all right, why isn't he here now?'

Momentarily ignoring her questions, the priest guided her firmly to the settee and stood over her, preventing her from getting back to her feet.

'Anthony's all right, nothing's happened to him – you have my word on it. He'll be home soon. They're bringing him back any moment, and he's not been harmed. I've seen him myself, and no one's laid a finger on him.'

She looked up into his face with suspicion, but his eyes met hers openly and bespoke a truth that she couldn't fail to recognise.

'But Father, why didn't he come back with you?' she asked, with dogged insistence.

'They're still talking to the boy, but they'll be bringing him home very soon.'

The priest sat down on a chair opposite her. He pushed back his hair with a sweep of his hand. His face was still flushed and a little glimmer of moisture trickled from his left eye. There were spots of mud on his shoes. She searched for answers to the questions which ricocheted round her head like a pin-ball.

'What is it they're talking to him about? Why did they take him away like that? What do they want with my boy?'

The priest shrunk back uneasily in the chair, contracting into it, his hands washing slowly over each other. For a second, his eyes lingered on the splashes of mud on his shoes, then he looked her in the face.

'They're talking to Anthony about what they call "anti-social activities" – break-ins and stealings, things like that.'

'Break-ins and stealings? My son hasn't been involved in anything like that. I know he hasn't, Father, and I'll go and tell them that as well.'

She started to rise from the settee but he raised a hand quickly to stop her.

'It's no use, Eilish, the boy's admitted it. He's confessed everything. All the pensioners' bungalows – he did them all. And a lot more besides. They've written it all down and he's signed it. They showed me it.'

'Of course he's signed it!' she shouted, her voice quivering with anger and fear. 'They've scared the boy half to death and you tell me he's signed some bit of paper. There's not many who wouldn't do the same with a gun pointed to their head.'

'There's no guns involved, and the boy hasn't been harmed. That's something we can be grateful for at least.'

'Grateful? They've taken a son away from his mother and you say we should be grateful! What right've they got to go round terrorising innocent families?'

She felt her anger flowing from her soul and she could not turn it anywhere but towards the priest. He had failed to bring her son back to her when she had placed all her faith in him, and now he talked of gratitude.

'Did you not talk to them, Father? Did you not tell them about me being a widow and struggling here on me own to bring up the boy?'

'I told them, Eilish – I told them everything – but it made no difference. There's no talking to thon fellows. The day's long gone when they'll listen to the likes of me.'

The priest slumped back into the chair and his voice was edged with a bright thread of bitterness.

'You could talk till you're blue in the face and they wouldn't listen. Once I could've made them see some sense but not now. There's no respect for God, nor man, any more. And there's Sean Walshe – a boy I baptised and confirmed with me own hand – talking to me with as much respect as you'd show to a dog. I've had a time of it, all right, one that I'll not forget in a hurry.'

But she could find no sympathy to spare for his feelings, or time to worry about them. Her mind was torn apart by twisted images of shattered kneecaps and broken limbs, of young men tarred and feathered and tied to railings with their crimes listed around their necks for all the world to see. A vision of the new stigmata – the dark red circles of bullet holes in the palms and thighs – imprinted itself on her cracking mind like a scourging crown of thorns. Holy Mother of God, who herself suffered so much, pity her now, pity her now.

'What are they going to do with him? In the name of God, tell me what they're going to do with my boy. I have to know. Are they going to hurt him? I have to know now!'

'They're not going to hurt him – I've told you that, and it was the truth, but it wasn't all the truth. I'm sorry Eilish, I'm very sorry, but I have to tell you something that's going to be very hard, and may God give you the grace to bear it.'

The priest paused for a second and looked at the spots of mud on his shoes. There was no easy way, but it had to be done.

'They've given him forty-eight hours to leave the city. If he's not packed and gone within that time, they'll come looking for him.'

She said nothing, but stared at him with empty eyes, as if not fully understanding the words she had heard. He leaned forward and stretched out his hand towards her in a gesture of comfort and support, but she sat motionless, almost unaware of his presence.

'Leave the city,' she whispered. 'Leave his mother and his home? How in the name of God can they say that?'

She continued to stare at the priest, desperately searching his face for some sign that he had made a mistake, or that she had misunderstood his words.

'He's no more than a boy – how can they do this to no more than a boy? Where will he go? What will become of him? And me – what's to become of me? God in heaven knows, I've little enough in this world and they're going to take away the one thing

I've got left. I don't care what he's done, or what he hasn't done, he's my son and no one has the right to do this. What gives the likes of them the right to be judge, jury and executioner? Did you not tell them that, Father? Did you not make them listen to you? People respect Father Donnelly round here, people listen to you.'

The priest sat back again in the chair, and felt the bitterness of his humiliation burn him again.

'I tried, Eilish, I really tried, but these people are a law unto themselves, and to them I'm just an old man with old ideas. They pushed me aside like some old fool who didn't understand. These are terrible times we're living in, and this is a terrible thing they're doing, but these people don't want to listen to reason. And why should they? Yesterday, they were nobodies, and today they sit in judgment on the world. They told me they were being lenient with the boy – giving him a chance when there were some who wanted to make an example of him.'

'But they can't do this,' she insisted. 'He's only a boy, where would he go? A boy isn't some sort of bird that can flit from nest to nest. Anthony may not be the best son any mother ever had, but he's mine and he's all I have. They can't take him away from me. In the name of Jesus, you can't let them do this!'

She got up and stumbled into the kitchen as the priest started to talk of people he knew south of the border who could provide accommodation and maybe even a job, and how the church would stand by her and help them both in every way possible, but his words blurred and circled aimlessly in her head before sinking slowly into futility. She searched frantically for the cigarette packet and the few remaining cigarettes but could not find it. She had hidden it and could not remember where. Soon there would be no need for hiding places, no need for anything any more.

Her eye fixed on the milk jug which occupied pride of place on the tray and she cupped it carefully in her hands. She had always loved the coolness of the blue flowers against the white, and her fingers gently traced the delicate pattern. Then, as a surge of savage tears broke inside her, she smashed it into the yellow-stained sink and watched it crack and shatter before her splintered sight. The sound made the priest start, and for a second he thought of going to her, but he slumped back heavily into the chair and stared morosely into the smouldering fire, as if searching it for some flicker of flame.

THE RED KITE

It was supposed to be a special treat. However, he was old enough to know that happiness was elusive and could not be pre-arranged. He saw, too, that the signs were not good. When his father first told him that they were going for a drive that Saturday, the prospect had pleased him, but his father's insistent and repetitive assurances about how good it would be sowed doubt in his mind. His mother exuded indifference. He wondered for whose benefit the trip had been arranged.

There had been something wrong in the house for a week, but he did not know what it was, and he was not old enough to ask. Several times, after he had gone to bed the sound of raised voices had carried to his room, but he had not been able to hear clearly enough to follow what was being said. He knew it was something to do with his father by the way he tried so hard to please and because his mother responded sullenly, almost resentfully. When she set his father's meal on the table, she set it down with ill grace, and when she lifted it up, it was as if she was going to throw the plate away. In his presence neither said anything about what was on their minds, and his father filled the silences with forced jocularity that fell hopelessly flat. It was as if the whole house was shrouded in some nameless and indefinable misery that seeped stealthily into every corner.

When Saturday arrived it was a cold September day that seemed to belong more to the coming winter than to the fading summer. His mother wrapped sandwiches in a greaseproof paper bag and placed them with a flask in a large white polythene bag. It was entrusted to his custody in the back seat of the car and he was told to make sure the flask didn't topple over and start to leak. He liked it best when he sat in the front with his father, but this time he was assigned to the back. Sometimes his father would say, 'Men in the front, women in the back.' But not this time. His mother checked her make-up in the little vanity mirror behind the passenger's sun-shield and they set off.

No one said much. His father drove steadily and his mother looked at houses as they passed. From time to time she turned round to make sure the flask was all right. It made him feel that she didn't trust him. His father began to talk about the old days and the old gang he had hung around with. He told them about the time they went camping in the Mournes and how the tent had blown away the first night. He told the stories he had told a score of times before. In spite of herself, his mother was laughing at them, just the way she always did. As his father drove, he glanced at her from time to time, as if to assure himself that it was really her laughter he was hearing. Once, almost as an afterthought, he glanced in his mirror to see if his son was laughing.

After a while they left the main roads and drove through the countryside. Looking out at the empty fields he found it difficult to associate the land with the people who made their living from it, and there was a featureless similarity in weather and landscape that made the whole world take on a kind of indistinguishable oneness. His father had run out of funny stories now, and silence had settled once more. They were driving quite slowly and the lanes were narrow. A car appeared behind them. It followed closely for a few miles and then the driver grew impatient with his inability to pass. He came even closer until the two cars were almost nose to tail. His father made no effort to pull over, but obstinately hugged the middle of the road. An angry horn sounded and his father asked with heavy sarcasm, 'Where's the fire? Where's the fire?' His mother glanced over her shoulder and told him to let the man past. His father made no attempt to comply at first, but sensing his wife's growing annoyance, he steered the car over towards the verge. There was another angry blast of horn as the car overtook them. His mother turned her head away and stared at the hedge, while his father glared at the driver. There was a little imitation dog sitting in the back of the other car, and as it disappeared into the distance the dog wagged its head at them with repeated scorn.

Feeling a vague sense of guilt, his father tried to justify himself.

'These young fellows think they own the roads.'

'He only wanted past,' his mother said flatly.

'I was going to let him past until he started pumping that horn. Wonder what else he got for Christmas?'

As he said this, he turned round to see if his son had appreciated the joke. His mother seemed to want to make an issue of it.

'He might have been in a hurry,' she insisted. 'Why should everyone have to wait on your beck and call?'

There was a reply on his father's lips, but he let it slip away unsaid and pretended to be concentrating on his driving.

Eventually they arrived in the small seaside town. The afternoon was cold with a strong wind blowing and few people on the streets. Most of the seafront shops were already closed and boarded-up for the winter. They found a place to park where they could sit and look at the sea. After a while they had their picnic, and it all seemed to be over too quickly. His father gave him twenty pence and told him to go and buy some sweets. As he got out of the car his mother began to busy herself with gathering up the papers and the cups. His father turned sideways and watched her.

There was only one shop open – the type that sold everything, and it appeared strange and out of place. Outside, it had buckets and spades hanging in the doorway and cowboy hats and brightly coloured beach balls. There was even a rack of postcards. The wind was blowing and some of the things seemed likely to blow away at any minute. He looked in the windows but did not go in. Then he slipped down on to the beach.

The sea was whipped by the wind into an angry lather of foam and noise, and the waves broke so quickly he could not count them. Huddled at the bottom of the steps and the base of the wall was a girl in a duffle coat with the hood up and a long, green scarf wrapped around her neck. On her knees was a large sketch pad and she was drawing a view of the rocks and sea. She had long, black hair which blew across her face, and she had to keep pushing it back with one hand, while holding on to the sketch pad with the other. He walked along the beach. A woman was walking her dog and as she went she threw a stick for it to fetch. Sometimes she threw it into the sea and the water rippled up round the dog's paws. On some rocks a man was fishing. He stood upright and motionless like a pole and didn't seem to be catching anything.

The boy began to skim stones but he couldn't find any really flat, smooth ones, and in the rough sea didn't manage more than two skips. Then he remembered the two coins his father had given him. He took them out and looked at them for a while. They were worn and soiled. With the second one he got four clear skims.

Further on, about fifty yards away, he saw two young boys with a kite. The kite seemed to be made of cloth and was bright red in colour. He went closer and crouched down in the sand against the sea-wall to watch them. They were standing together, holding the kite between them and conferring about something. Everything seemed to be going wrong for them. First of all the string became ravelled and it took them about five minutes to sort it out. They were using one of those green fishing lines on a square wooden frame. Eventually, they sorted it out and one walked backwards holding the kite in his right hand, sometimes almost stumbling when his boots sunk into a patch of soft sand. The other boy stood still, letting out the line and keeping it taut. Then, when they were both in position, the boy with the kite lifted it with both hands to head height and threw it into the air. His friend began pulling frantically on the string and moving backwards, but it was no use. The kite rose to a height of about thirty feet and then lurched sideways in a crazy spin that brought it crashing to the ground. Even then the wind would not let it go but grabbed it by the hair and kicked it along the beach, snapping and snarling at its heels, and as he watched it bounce and trail along the sand, he thought the frame would break.

But the frame did not break, and when the two boys recovered it they changed places and tried again. Their second attempt had no more success than the first. Once again, thé kite veered out of control to the left and crashed to the ground, as if pulled by a magnet. The wind caught it and trailed it along. The boy holding the string fell over in his efforts to keep the line taut and the other chased after it, holding his woollen cap on with one hand.

When the kite had been retrieved and the line untangled and wound in, they conferred again. This time the boy holding the kite walked to the sea-wall and stood facing out, while his partner let out the line carefully and stood with his back to the sea. Then, just as a strong breeze blew in, the kite was released, this time soaring skyward like a bird. It was up, it was really up, hooked tight on the wind, tugging and reeling at the line. Higher and higher it climbed, rippling and swooping in a drunken breeze. Its tail danced dizzily like a swirling, magic serpent. The boy felt a thrill of excitement shoot through him. Then, silently crouching down in the sand, he thought of his mother and father sitting in the car, and wished they would look up, if only people would look up at this red kite, everyone would be cured and everything would be well.

ON THE SHORE

STRAIGHTENING IN his chair, he looked down the five rows of desks. Mary Blair's pencil case would fall soon. She sat rule-breaking, with one leg curled beneath her on the seat, her tongue peeping out of the corner of her mouth as she wielded a broken stub of a pencil. He despised the clumsiness which left her oblivious to her elbow pushing the pencil case to the edge of the desk. It was heavy and wooden, and when it fell it would make a great noise. A boy at the back of the room coughed and then raised his eyes in an apology. Thomas Murray was showing his companion something under the desk, but he would not break the silence for one stupid boy. There would be opportunity for punishment later.

It would soon be time to inspect their work. But not just yet. He settled into the seat again and for the hundredth time that day, despite all his inner protests, he allowed his gaze to rest on her empty desk. And then, almost involuntarily, his eyes swept to the back wall, to where her painting was. The flowers were all wrong – they were too big and too brightly coloured in red, green and yellow. They weren't like real flowers. Against the prim neatness of the wall, they stood out like a beacon. They were too bright. It had been foolish to put them up and he would take them down as soon as the end of school came. That would not be long now. The directness of his resolution reassured him, and he drew strength from it, but it was only a temporary respite, and soon it slowly faded away like the afternoon sun. His eyes returned to the empty desk. He tried not to think about her. He marked some books, sorted some papers on his desk, totalled the monthly roll, but at every turn her face seeped through the dead weight of ritual with which he tried to block her out. He grew impatient and angry with himself, but even then the anger dissolved itself into a feeling he did not know the name of and whose strangeness brought him confusion and a little fear. He straightened in his chair again. Mary Blair's pencil case slipped closer to the edge of the desk. Another few inches and it would fall. From the back of the room the flowers burned his eyes. He closed them and thought about her.

There had been interruptions all afternoon, and this latest one annoyed him. He snapped the piece of paper out of the messenger's hand. It was from the headmaster, asking if he could come to his office for a few minutes at the end of school. The messenger stood still with an expressionless face, neither smiling at his friends nor doing anything that could merit reprimand. He stared into the boy's face until he lowered his eyes to the floor, then gave a curt nod to signify that he had read and understood the note. The boy stood on.

'Are you going to stand there all day?'

'Please sir, Mr Elliot asked me to wait for a reply.'

'Tell Mr Elliot I can give him a few minutes.'

The boy turned and left the room, carefully closing the door behind him so that it did not bang. He wondered what the headmaster wanted. He half wished that the note had told him to come, so that he could have announced a prior engagement, or that it was not convenient, but Elliot knew better than to take that approach with him. It had been a request, not a directive. In all the years he had been in the school, he could barely remember Elliot giving him a direct order. It wasn't a question of politeness, because he had often seen Elliot play the headmaster with the younger women teachers – he had even seen one girl reduced to tears. But that was typical of Elliot, always aiming at the weakest targets, happy to take advantage of those who would let him. He almost wished he would try it on with him, but there was little chance of that – Elliot didn't have the backbone. All he had was his fawning mediocrity, and yet Elliot held a position he himself would never hold. He had made too many enemies, had said the right things at the wrong times, had not cultivated influence in the right circles, and had won no patronage. Vice-principal in a city primary school was to be the pinnacle of his career. Now that he had reached that pathetic little position, there was nowhere for him to go, and the knowledge of it stung him with its bitterness. He tried to draw some consolation from the fact that he had always been his own man, but the thought of the spineless Elliot surged again and vanquished the little solace he had managed to summon.

The end-of-school bell would ring soon. With a nod of his head, he set the packing-up process in motion. The pupils at the head of each row collected their assigned items, a tall boy cleaned the blackboard, another closed the open windows, while two girls gave out homework books. It was all over in a minute. They sat with their arms folded, bags on desks and waited in silence for the bell to ring. When it sounded, he nodded again. A boy went over to the door as the class rose, put their seats under the desks and stood in the space where the seats had been. Another nod. The boy opened the door and the row nearest filed out, followed in sequence by the other rows. After the last person in the last row had left, the boy followed, closing the door behind.

As he locked the drawers of his desk and set his own chair underneath it, he wondered what it was Elliot wanted with him. It couldn't be a general staff meeting and it couldn't be a meeting to discuss policy. The thought of policy meetings made him smile. Every so often, Elliot would have his head filled with some new half-baked idea from one of his headmaster cronies, usually in the golf-club bar, or at a one-day conference, and then feel obliged to pass it on to his vice-principal. He would receive it with barely concealed indifference, and then go on teaching in the way he had always done. Anyway, his results stood for all to see. Each year, he had a good percentage of examination passes and subsequent entrances to the grammar school. If Elliot thought anyone else could improve on his record, they were welcome to try; indeed, the more he thought about it, the more he suspected that he was growing a little weary of the examination class – too much trying to get blood out of stones, too much pushing, and too many parents with inflated opinions of their child's ability. Of course, he wouldn't give up the class without a struggle. Let Elliot try to take it away from him and he would fight him every step of the way, but all the same, perhaps in a few years' time he himself might choose to relinquish the burden. Not that there was any natural successor waiting in the wings – just a series of young women teachers who stayed for three or four years and then moved on or started families. Below him there were only Mrs Simpson and Miss Sharp, who had been there seven years, and neither of them was up to taking the examination class.

He closed the classroom door and as he turned to walk down the corridor, he was confronted by a boy in full flight. The boy came to an instant halt but the expression on his face showed that he knew he had been seen running.

'Well?'

Silence.

'Well, boy, I'm waiting for you to explain to me why you were running in the corridor.'

Silence.

'You do know that you're not allowed to run in the corridor?'

'Yes, sir.'

He raised his voice suddenly.

'Well, then, why were you doing it?'

The boy continued to shelter in silence.

'What is your name? Whose class are you in?'

'Stephen Weir, sir. Miss Osborne's class.'

'And why are you only going home now?'

'Miss Osborne kept me in, sir.'

'Kept in, no doubt, for misbehaving and the moment you're let out you proceed to break one of the school rules by running in the corridor. I don't like this, Weir – I don't like it at all. I shall be keeping an eye on you, young man, and if I come across you again, I'll give you something to remember me by. Do you understand?'

'Yes, Mr Andrews.'

'Now – on your way.'

He stood and watched until the boy had walked the full length of the corridor. It pleased him that the boy had used his name, reassuring him that his reputation still flourished throughout the school. It was something he took every care to preserve and perpetuate, and was an important weapon in his armoury. Once set in motion, it was not difficult to keep it rolling, and so it went before him and prepared his way. Yet it was a reputation based on nothing other than solid fact, and acknowledged by the many children who had sat in his classes. Too many children. He grew weary of them.

As he passed Miss Osborne's class, he looked in through the window. She was keeping in five boys – five reprobates by the look of them. They were spaced round the room, but by their insolent postures and casual signalling to each other, it was obvious she was being punished, rather than they. One was flicking a piece of paper at another, but as soon as his presence was realised, the five slipped into the roles of model pupils, while she reddened and pretended not to see him. It was always embarrassing for people to be confronted by their inadequacies, but he had no sympathy for her, or her incompetence. They came out of college, young slips of girls, armed with naive enthusiasm and ideas given to them by people who knew nothing about real children, and who spent their careers avoiding them, then floundered against difficult, unco-operative children, who possessed the strength of numbers and weight of ignorance. He would mention Miss Osborne to Elliot; after all, as headmaster he was being paid good money to deal with problems like this. He wondered again what Elliot wanted with him.

With a cursory knock at the office door, he briskly entered the room. Elliot was standing in front of his desk, smiling blandly.

'Ah, Mr Andrews, good of you to come at such short notice.'

The inane smile seemed fixed on his face as his left hand stretched forward in a gesture of welcome. There were two other people and a child in the room. Elliot's gush of geniality and the school's best china teaset suggested that the guests were considered to be of some importance.

105

'Mr Andrews, I would like you to meet Mr and Mrs Lawrenson, and their daughter, Lysandra.'

They shook hands, and as he turned to acknowledge the child with a nod of his head, he realised, to his discomfort, that she was stepping towards him with her hand outstretched. For a second he thought of pretending that he did not see it, but there was no trace of hesitancy, of self-consciousness, in her movement that might allow this. There was no avenue of escape. He raised his hand limply and as she shook it he glanced at Elliot, but could discern no perceptible change in his expression. The couple were in their late thirties. He was originally from the city, but was lecturing in a university in England and had come back on some sort of year's exchange scheme. Rather than split the family, it had been decided that his wife and daughter should accompany him. The girl had already been accepted for a place in a public school when they returned again. Elliot obviously considered them a great catch, and something of a feather in his personal cap. He himself was less enthusiastic in his response. As soon as he had heard that Lawrenson was involved in education, he felt a foreboding based on past experience. Parents who thought they knew something about the educational process were the worst possible type – always asking for interviews, sending letters of complaint, always trying to steer the boat from the shore. They also seemed collectively incapable of admitting the possibility that educationally successful parents might not have particularly brilliant children. It would help him a little if the girl was bright, but he supposed that it was merely a matter of time before the pleasant Mr and Mrs Lawrenson became his educational critics, pouring scorn on supposedly old-fashioned methods and aims, and quoting the latest reports and papers. This couple were potentially more troublesome than any he had faced before. It was already obvious that Elliot considered them as something approaching illustrious patrons, and he was not likely to treat their criticisms lightly, nor have their opinions dismissed with disdain.

Of course, if Elliot had possessed any backbone, he wouldn't have permitted parents over the front door of the school in the first instance. There was no place for them, or their complaints or advice. They wouldn't think for a moment of advising the baker how to bake bread, or the carpenter how to saw wood, but as soon as it came to educating their child, they inevitably presumed that they could influence and direct the process. If he had a pound for every parent he had put in their place, he would have been able to retire in luxury. Elliot was worse than useless. In the face of an irate parent, he would adopt a placatory attitude, a benign neutrality, and hope to offer enough sympathy to pacify the supposed grievance. He himself usually adopted a reciprocal attitude to his complainant. If they were polite and respectful, he would be the same, and try his best to explain whatever it was they needed explained, but the moment they became aggressive or presumptuous he would give better than he got. He felt tempted to smile as he thought of the adversaries sent away with their tails between their legs. It was never really much of a contest, and even if under some pressure, or merely if he grew impatient, he could always play his trump card and, with a tone of casual dismissal, inform them that if they were unhappy with their child's education, they were perfectly at liberty to take them elsewhere. It always gave him pleasure to say that in front of Elliot.

This particular meeting, however, only lasted a short time. A few pleasant generalities were exchanged on both sides, and Elliot made a joke about the poor Irish weather, while the Lawrensons described some of the hazards involved in moving house. He helped Elliot out on a few occasions with a couple of questions about Mr Lawrenson's particular subject and career. It was all over in fifteen minutes. The girl would join his class on Monday, and if any problems should arise, they encouraged him to contact them. Both sides assured each other that such an event was unlikely, then, as they were leaving, Mrs Lawrenson had an afterthought.

'Mr Elliot, I forgot to ask, does Lysandra need a school uniform?'

He enjoyed Elliot's embarrassed fluster as he momentarily struggled for an answer.

'No, Mrs Lawrenson, not necessary. We don't have a uniform – we try as much as possible to encourage individuality in the children, and we've tried to get away from the uniformity syndrome.'

That was a good one. The school never had a uniform simply because Elliot had neither the drive nor the interest to create one. As vice-principal he had suggested its introduction on numerous occasions, and each time it had been conveniently shelved for future consideration, or dismissed as a low priority. Anything that needed energy or the application of discipline was a low priority to Elliot. A round of golf followed by a round of drinks seemed to be the highest peak of human activity his soul aspired to.

After the Lawrensons had left, he thought of raising the question again, but a glance at his watch told him that he was late. The two men's sudden awareness of each other in the tiny office forced them into small talk.

'Well, they seemed quite a nice couple,' said Elliot, looking at him for confirmation.

'Yes. He seemed young to be a university lecturer.'

'They get younger all the time – or is it just that we're getting older? By the way, how's your father keeping?'

'He's not doing so badly, thank you,' he replied quickly.

There was always something in him that shied away from discussions that involved his father. Elliot had only asked out of politeness, but he balked at revealing the problems he faced in his world that existed outside school. Taking up his bag, he left Elliot's office and walked out through the front doors of the school. Going through the front gates, he noticed a boy's head drop down behind a parked car, and without staring or looking near him, he knew it belonged to the boy he had spoken to in the corridor. Weir, Miss Osborne's class. Waiting for his friends. He filed away the name in his memory. He had lied to Elliot about his father. For some reason he wasn't sure of, he always had – maybe he was just too proud to let anyone offer him sympathy; maybe it went against his strongly held belief that people should take responsibility for whatever situation they found themselves in, and get on quietly with their lives, avoiding fuss or drama.

The car engine wouldn't start. Pulling out the choke, it spluttered into unenthusiastic life after bronchial coughing and wheezing, and as the car pulled away, he looked in his mirror and saw Weir standing up and staring after him. But he thought no more about the boy. He always enjoyed the fifteen minutes' drive it took to reach home. The rush hour traffic was still an hour away, and sometimes, by driving slowly and precisely, he managed to savour the time. He enjoyed the pure mechanical response of the car, the immediacy and physical supremacy of his wordless control. The journey acted as a buffer between school and home. That day, it seemed to pass too quickly. He wondered what sort of day his father had had, but as he drew up in the driveway and looked up at the house it gave no clues. It stood in its quiet suburban avenue, indistinct and silent, distinguishable from its neighbours only by its own personalised veneer of shabbiness. The green paint had grown darker over the years – in places it looked black – and the garden was losing all traces of its former glory. His father was no longer able to tend it and there was little hint of the splendour he had once maintained. He himself had no talent for it, but he resolved to spend some time that weekend in tidying it up. If it was warm enough, his father could sit and watch him, and he would be pleased at the chance to issue advice and instructions. It was a good idea.

As he walked to the front door he looked in at the sitting room. On the piano that no one had ever played sat his parents' wedding photograph, and a photograph of himself, taken at his graduation ceremony. The room was never used now, except on those rare occasions when visitors called, and even then he suspected that it required something of an effort on their parts to sit in it for any length of time. He started to look for his key, but stopped when he saw the front door was partly opened. Mrs Mitchell was standing in the hallway. She was wearing her coat and was in the middle of putting on her headscarf, a bad sign.

'It's a quarter past four, Mr Andrews.'

'Yes, I'm sorry, Mrs Mitchell.'

'I should have been away fifteen minutes ago.'

She bristled with indignation, drawing her favourite shawl of the exploited about her.

'Yes, I know, Mrs Mitchell. Mr Elliot wanted a word after school. I'm sorry I'm late.'

Her annoyance had abated, but she realised that she held a strong position and was determined to make the most of it. She continued, 'Fifteen minutes mightn't seem very much, but if I was to come fifteen minutes late in the morning it would hardly do, would it?'

In her two-year spell as home-help, they had often crossed swords, and at times he had spoken sharply, but on this occasion he was in no mood for a fight. He remained silent as she drained the last dregs from her grievance.

'It's not because I'm not getting paid for it, Mr Andrews – you know I don't do it for the money. But if I'm not home, Jim's tea won't be on the table when he comes in, and I don't like the boys being alone too long in the house. I tell them to get their homeworks done when they come in from school, but you never know what mischief they might be getting up to. I'm sure you understand that.'

'I understand, Mrs Mitchell. It won't happen again. You know I'd run you home in the car if it was possible.'

'That's all right – I'm not looking for a lift.'

She checked her headscarf in the hall mirror and gathered up her umbrella and shopping bag, then turned and looked at his father, who was sitting in an armchair facing the window.

'I'm off now, Mr Andrews. See you on Monday.'

She did not wait for a reply and none came. He held open the front door for her as she hurried down the hall.

'What sort of day did you have?' he asked.

She paused only when she was outside the house.

'Just the normal. Not too bad, really. All the usual complaints of course, but he didn't want to go out or anything.'

She had already started off down the drive as she spoke these last few words, leaving him to stare at the back of her head. The headscarf she was wearing had pictures of Paris printed on it. He closed the door and went into the living room, resolving not to be late again. For all her faults, the woman was reliable and satisfactory home-helps were not easy to come by. She tolerated his father and had become accustomed to his ways. They too had become accustomed to her. The prospect of losing her and having to find, and introduce, some stranger, frightened him a little. He would not be late again.

'Well, had a good day?'

His father grunted a reply that seemed to ridicule the question.

'That woman has no business coming here. She acts as if she owns the house. Acts as if she owns it. We don't need her here, touching things and prying into things that don't concern her.'

He knew his father's speech by heart, having listened to it at regular intervals for two years, and as always he ignored it.

'Come on, let's move you over here and I'll put the television on.'

He bent over and helped his father to raise himself, feeling the staleness of his breath upon his face. Experience taught him the importance of letting it appear that his father was helping himself, and he disguised his own effort as best he could. With slow, sidling steps, they moved over to the armchair in front of the electric fire and facing the television. He lowered his father gently down into the depths of his chair and then found a cushion to support his back. The operation took several minutes. When it was over, he switched on the television. Children's programmes were just starting, and he knew that there was a good chance his father would sit watching them for the next hour, giving him time to prepare the evening meal. It was usually something light and simple, restricted as always by the limitations of his range, but it didn't really matter so much as Mrs Mitchell made his father a hot meal each midday, and he took his own lunch in the school dining-centre. Since his father's condition had deteriorated she came twice a day – a period in the morning and a shorter period in the afternoon. Recently, he had started to pay her more and she was staying for longer, arriving in the morning when it was time for him to leave for school, leaving after she had prepared the midday meal, then returning again from two to four o'clock. His father's decreasing mobility made him reliant on someone's help, and if it wasn't a perfect solution, it was the best that could be done under the circumstances.

From time to time he came out of the kitchen and looked in at his father as he sat watching television. A woman was making doll's furniture out of cardboard. He brought the meal in and they ate it off trays while his father continued watching. When it was eaten he returned to the kitchen and brought in two mugs of tea. His father cupped his in both hands under his chin and the steam curtained his face – sometimes it seemed as if he took more pleasure from its warmth against his skin than from its taste. They sat in silence. The tea cooled. His father began to drink it in noisy slurps like a child taking soup. A man on the television was balancing a plate on one finger.

'I thought of tidying the garden tomorrow if the weather's good.'

'It's going to rain. Do you not see the sky?'

'Tomorrow might be all right. You could sit out and advise me what to do.'

His father stopped drinking and turned his head towards him. A rivulet of moisture ran down the side of his mouth and his eyes were blue-bagged and tired.

'Sure the garden's dead. It's a bit late in the day to be asking for advice.'

There was an edge of bitterness in his voice that seeped into the atmosphere and smothered the possibility of future conversation. He took his cup into the kitchen and began to wash up. His father would hold his empty cup until the last vestige of heat had gone out of it.

His father had become a problem. He had never really recovered from the death of his wife, and while the immediate pain of grief had faded, it had been replaced by a bitter, bewildered emptiness. After her death the house had died too, and they had become like strangers whose lives were locked together. It must always have been like that, only hidden from them by the business of living. She had been the hub of their lives, uniting them both in her, and when she died they floundered, helpless and apart, having to learn new patterns and follow paths that were foreign to them. In the months after her death they had come to some unspoken arrangement and tried, together, to do the best they could, but the further they moved away from it, the more things fell apart. They shadow-boxed in the shell house, engaged in little contests of will over matters and objects which, though trivial in themselves, assumed epic proportions. The honours had been evenly shared until the battle of the sitting room, which his father had wanted to preserve exactly the way she had always kept it, out of respect to her memory, while he wanted to have it redecorated. He found forgetting a better salve for grief, but his father had won in the end and so the room sat like a mausoleum, uncared for and unused. A layer of dust fell on the china cabinet, the unplayed piano, the lace covers, the photographs, and coated every object in the room. Mrs Mitchell, aware of his father's wish, was happy on this occasion to comply and completely ignored it.

The intensity of battle had frightened them both a little, and both sides had inflicted wounds that festered for months. When it was over, they stepped back a little, and moved into a period of measured restraint. They lived in a functional way as each learned to tolerate the other, and while little frictions arose occasionally at those points where their routines crossed, neither side sought to inflict defeat upon the other. A wordless accommodation was reached and they co-existed in an almost satisfactory way. As his father grew older he found himself more prepared to defer to his wishes, especially in areas which no longer seemed important, but his father's illness had altered the balance of their relationship, and with his decreasing mobility had come an increasing depend-ence on his son. Although it was never spoken of they both knew it was so, and although they both pretended that nothing had changed, each knew that the father had relinquished mastership of the house. During the slow process of his father's abdication, he was always at pains to maintain an outward display of deference, but both knew as he moved gently through their lives, leaving behind only a snail-trail of his will, that the struggle was over. Coupled in recent years with his physical failing had come a gradual mental deterioration, manifested at first in small things such as failing memory and then a slide into periods of confusion and incoherence. In the last few months these periods had grown longer and the gaps between them shorter. At other times, however, his mind seemed clear and well. He knew that the arrangement with Mrs Mitchell was not going to be adequate if his father's mental deterioration continued, and it might eventually prove impossible for him to be left on his own. In the meantime, they must make the best of the situation. Weekends were especially difficult. Mrs Mitchell did not come and so they were both bound together in an ever diminishing range of activities. His idea about the garden had been a good one. In spite of his father's prediction, it did not rain, and the next morning he helped him outside and eased him into an armchair brought from the house. His father settled into a mood of pained scepticism as he watched him cut the grass and pull out some of the more obvious weeds. He made a half-hearted attempt to prune the roses, but he wasn't sure of what he was doing, while throughout the morning his father contented himself with criticism after the completion of each operation. As he worked he thought of school and the new girl. There were thirty-six pupils in his class and she would make thirty-seven. He disliked the unevenness of the number. Should he give her a seat beside Grace Maxwell or Ann Brown? Ann Brown – she was a sensible girl who would induct the new arrival into the routines and rules. He tried to remember clearly what she looked like, but he was unable to picture her with any great conviction.

On that first Monday morning after assembly, Elliot escorted her round to his room. He went to the door to meet them both, and with a nod of his head thanked Elliot, his brusque manner discouraging him from entering the room. The girl stepped diffidently into the room as the class looked up from their work and stared silently at her. He closed the classroom door and in the silence Elliot's footsteps could be heard echoing down the corridor. She turned and looked at him with an expression that seemed to ask for directions. He showed her to the seat beside Ann Brown. The two girls smiled at each other. Taking the opportunity to observe her, he was struck by how much she resembled her mother. She was of average height and had shoulder-length black hair tied back in two pigtails and fastened with red plastic clips. Her eyes were brown and when she smiled they seemed to smile as well. As he inspected her, he was pleased to see that her parents had dressed her suitably. She was dressed simply in a navy blue cardigan over a white blouse with a blue pleated skirt. Her socks were white and she wore red shoes with a strap and small silver buckles. She had though that fine sheen of health that marked the children of the well-off. She carried with her a small, brown leather schoolbag, and a few seconds after she sat down, she took from it a plastic pencil case shaped like an elephant, and put it on the desk in front of her. The children stared at her and at the pencil case. Any nervousness she might have had appeared to have evaporated and she seemed calm and self-possessed as he introduced her to the class. He told them only her name, where she came from, and that she was joining the class. The girls stared at her black hair with its two red clasps, and those boys who could see it stared at the pencil case. As he spoke her name, he listened to its sound. Lysandra. It was a stupid name for a child. He resented having to say it – it sounded absurd on his lips and out of place in his room. It suggested the pretension that he sought so keenly to discourage in children. Saying the name was almost an embarrassment to him – as if he had been caught in public wearing a garish tie or a striped shirt, and when he wrote it on the roll below the names of the other girls, its incongruity irritated him. Susan Walker, Arlene Wells, Jean Young, Lysandra Lawrenson. For a second he thought of breaking with his lifelong practice of calling the girl pupils by their Christian names and boys by their surnames, but he refused to let the foolishness of one set of parents disrupt his habits.

Other than supplying her at intervals with the necessary books, he paid her no further personal attention. It was a bad thing to make a fuss of children, giving them an inflated opinion of their own importance and distracting them from the learning process. While parents might think themselves enlightened in giving full rein to their children's individuality, he had often witnessed the results as spoilt brats humiliated their parents in public places with calculated outbursts of tantrums and wilful defiance. Children were children and needed to be treated as such. He had often encountered adults who behaved like children, but never in all his years of teaching had he met children who behaved like adults. If anywhere in the world such phenomena existed, they were unhealthy and unnatural, and unworthy of emulation. He harboured no illusions and he built his philosophy on no other foundation than long experience. While each child might be different, their differences were unimportant, irrelevancies in the same way that a particular brand of car might come in different colours, what was important was their universal, knowable, mouldable similarity. When children were known for what they were, it was possible to teach them; when the numerous factors that constituted a child were understood, it was possible to direct them. There was certainly nothing in them that was mysterious or noble, or even particularly splendid – in that, at least, they were like adults.

He spent each day of his working life in a room with over thirty children. It amused him to listen to parents complaining about having difficulty coping with a single child on long holidays or wet days, and yet every day he was required to cope with that child and over thirty more. It had not taken him long to realise what that meant. In his first year out of college, he had come with an open mind and a great deal of energy. After the first year he had been exhausted and almost defeated. He had made mistakes, but he prided himself in the fact that he had never made the same one twice, and when he returned after the summer, he came armed with the weapons necessary for success. He had been fortunate that he was faced with a new class, and, starting with a clean slate, he had never looked back.

In any struggle for control the strongest would always win and from that day forward he had always been the strongest in his classroom. In the early years a few had sought to dispute that control, but he had cut them down like a scythe cuts the heads off wild flowers in a meadow. After a time, there were no more challengers. The moment that he had committed himself to the initial struggle there had never been any doubt as to its outcome – the need for victory was too important to him. One of the first things he had realised was that it was not possible to treat a class as individuals. It was a foolish and fantastic notion. To do so was to have your soul slowly eaten away like an army of ants scavenging at some dead carcass. No human being could struggle against thirty different temperaments, thirty individual wills and desires. It was a recipe for chaos – he had realised that. He could not struggle against so many, no one could, the odds were too great. And so he broke every class into one animal, one living unit over which his will dominated and exercised control. Without exception, every child was treated the same, and in that at least he was a true democrat. He set standards high enough to encapsulate sound values, but possible for each child to attain. He said nothing he did not mean, made no promises he did not keep, and no threats he did not carry out. He would cut off his hand before he would let his word lose credibility in the eyes of his class. His given word was holy writ. Against its rock hardness the waywardness of foolish pupils shipwrecked like little boats; under its steadfast shadow the frail vessels of the insecure moored, and found assurance in its solidity. Into these calm waters had sailed a new girl. He looked at her. She had a foolish name and a foolish pencil case, but that was all. She was working intently at her arithmetic and he was pleased at her diligence. He noticed the two red clips in her black hair and knew that she would stir no ripples, cause no waves.

It was three weeks later during an art lesson that the first doubt came. This lesson was not a favourite of his. Children and paint was a combination that easily resulted in mess despite whatever rigid regulations might be enforced. Although he had effectively reduced the opportunities for chaos, it was impossible to eliminate them completely. He would have been happy enough to spend the time in continual sketching, or crayon work, if he had not felt an obligation to use the paints each class was supplied with. He also disliked the time for another reason. Art gave the children opportunities to stray down paths and into areas where he had no role to play or experience to influence. It also involved him in unwelcome judgments of value and pleasure – whereas the majority of what a child presented him in the classroom could be easily identified and marked as right or wrong, their work in the art class demanded a different appraisal. It was an assessment he did not feel competent to give, and he was reluctant to enter into the relationship which he felt the bestowal of too generous approval would give.

On that particular day they had been doing half-drop repeat patterns. First of all the page was divided into squares of set measurement and then the pattern was repeated in each one. He had chosen flowers as the subject matter and restricted the number of colours to three. For the less able pupils, much of the time was spent in ruling the necessary squares and only the better ones were able to complete the exercise. It was obvious that his new pupil had completed her pattern. From the silent attention it was evoking from those close enough to see it, he realised that there was something special about it. His own curiosity rose a little. Getting up from his desk, he stopped and looked down over her shoulder. The flowers were enormous – each one was the size of a saucer. They were a blaze of red with green and yellow stems and the whole page was a burning splash of colour. Looking at them made him feel breathless. The children sitting close by were staring at them too, and waiting to hear what he would say. He felt the pressure to say something, but was unsure of what line to take.

'Lysandra, this was supposed to be a half-drop repeat. Did you not understand what that meant?'

'It is a half-drop repeat, Mr Andrews.'

As soon as she spoke he realised that she was right. But it was too late and he sensed the little ripple of satisfaction spreading over the surface of the class. He could not let go now.

'Yes, perhaps,' he conceded grudgingly, 'but the flowers are too big – your squares are the wrong size. Look at the measurements on the board.'

'I know, Mr Andrews. I made them that size at first, but the flowers didn't seem to fit, so I made the squares bigger.'

The reason behind the logic seemed unassailable, and the

resulting pattern impressed all those who could see it. He felt the need for a successful conclusion to the issue.

'Fitting the pattern into the measurements is part of the problem. It requires concentration – self-discipline if you like. Anyone can throw paint down on paper, but keeping a tight pattern is a more difficult thing.'

But it was obvious that not just anyone could have painted those red flowers. They were special. He felt he was struggling and tried to extricate himself.

'Instructions are important. If everyone only followed their own ideas, we'd soon be in a sorry mess. What would happen if the bus driver only drove his bus whenever it suited him, and not when the timetable said?'

His attempt at humour fell flat. It evoked no response and as he walked back to his desk, he felt a vague feeling of defeat. The paintings were collected by the pupils at the top of each row and placed in a cupboard reserved for art work. The girl at the top of Lysandra's row collected the paintings carefully, shuffling them so that the red flowers were top of the pile, and out of the corner of his eye he watched her quietly showing it to the other collectors as they queued to place their paintings in the cupboard. There was a touch of pride in her gesture, as if collecting it caused her to share its glory. His feeling of defeat grew sharper.

Without admitting it to himself, he punished them with an hour of mathematical problems which were just outside the ability range of most of the class, and even those who were successful in solving them did not escape the sharp edge of his tongue. The correct answer was not enough – the arrival at it had to be preceded by clearly demonstrated logical steps. A mass of untidy figures and calculations was merely an insult. Those who had mastered the problems felt they had been imprudent and began to regret straying from the anonymity of the herd. But there was no easy escape for the rest. He was irritated and the signs were there for all the class to read. Past experience told them to keep their heads down and draw hope from the fact that there was a good statistical chance that his temper would not blow itself out on them. Their very act of putting up the shutters and drawing into a tight collective little shell would anger him even more, but they knew no other way. He spoke to them in a series of questions, deadly in their simplicity and raw in the tone of his voice.

'Why can you not do these?'

Silence.

'What is it you don't understand?'

A bee buzzed against a window, bouncing off the glass. No one took their eyes off him. It roared like a plane and then escaped.

'Is it just sheer wooden-headedness?'

They stared at him with blank, motionless faces, and their minds raced with frantic calculations and eliminations. He was not to be placated. The worst would come now.

'Roberta Osbourne – come to the board!'

Their worst expectations were fulfilled. There was no sense of relief at not being chosen – each felt sympathy for the sacrifice to their collective guilt, and each knew that soon their name might be called. The lamb was the girl who had collected the painting of the red flowers. She walked quickly and submissively to the board, standing a foot away from it with her back to the class.

'Take the chalk. Write up the first problem.'

The girl followed the instructions like an automaton. Her handwriting seemed pitifully small on the expanse of black. It sloped acutely to one side.

'Take the duster, rub it out, and start again. Make your figures big enough for everyone to see please.'

The girl swallowed and fumbled with the duster. It slipped and clattered to the floor but she did not pick it up. The noise was terrible in their ears but it seemed to break the mood that had enveloped him. He knew the girl would cry soon and, walking over to her, he picked it up and cleaned the board.

'Now, Roberta, get the figures on the board.'

His voice was encouraging rather than menacing, and the girl responded as quickly and effectively as she could. When she had finished, he motioned her to one side, and there was relief in her face as she realised the moment had passed from her. He handed her the duster to hold and she stood like a magician's assistant, gripping it with both hands as if she had been given a sacred trust. His anger had gone now, but he continued with the same directness and force as before. He knew the impetus that fear gave to learning, and slowly and precisely he explained the method required, then gave copious examples on the board, each one laid out with meticulous care. When he had finished, he gestured the girl to sit down and stepped forward to the first row of desks.

'Now, get them done again. And get them right this time!'

As if a starting gun had sounded, heads dropped to their books and gave pursuit to the correct answers. The storm had passed and as he sat at his desk and watched them work he felt angry with himself for having disturbed his own calm. And though no head was raised to look at him, from the living, breathing heart of the silent class, he could feel the swell of hatred spreading slowly towards him. Then, in the stillness, he saw a head lift and look at him. It was his new pupil. He wondered why she was not frightened of him – it was true that she was new to the school and probably unaware of his reputation, that highly polished harbinger he cherished and encouraged, but there had been others before her who had also been new and from the start he had held them helpless in his hand. It wasn't that she was stupid, because sometimes stupid children required a greater effort than others. If anything, she was probably brighter than anyone in the class – it had not taken him long to realise that. That was a problem too. She had often finished tasks before others had realised what was required of them, and she displayed a keen and simmering curiosity that could not be smothered by indifference or snubbed by brusqueness. She did too, what no other child had ever done, and asked him questions, questions that were relevant and perceptive and required answers. They were asked politely and genuinely, out of a spirit of enquiry and not a desire to draw attention to herself. On many occasions, too, she followed a methodology that was foreign to him but impressive in its accuracy and directness. She sat now, looking up at him with an expression on her face that disconcerted him. There was curiosity in her eyes, but behind that, there was another emotion that he could put no name to, and one which he found vaguely unsettling. He stared down at her but she did not look away. A murmur of conversation at the side of the room distracted him, and when his gaze returned to where she was sitting, her head was down and she too was engrossed in her work.

In the subsequent weeks and months he watched her popularity spread through the class. There was something in her personality that the other children found attractive, an open, unassuming friendship that was offered to anyone prepared to accept it, and while she had many reasons to feel superior, there was no visible evidence of condescension. There was, too, a tomboyish quality about her that allowed her to participate in games that the boys had previously considered exclusively theirs, and while everything had originally suggested that the girl would be an outsider, her very differences admitted her to the heart of the class. He himself found his attention increasingly returning to her, and at first dismissed it as mere curiosity. Often, from the classroom window, he watched her in the centre of a cluster of children, and wondered about the discussion that was taking place. Once, in an empty classroom at lunchtime, he found himself surreptitiously examining her possessions, handling her pencil case, touching the pens and pencils, and looking at the contents of her schoolbag, until the sound of feet in the corridor made him start guiltily away. At other times, resentment against her led him to a deliberate neglect of her work and almost of her very presence.

Nevertheless, there were many occasions when her talents became the focal point of the class, and he felt himself relegated to the role of a spectator in his own class. One wet Tuesday afternoon, the class had gone to the central hall for their weekly recorder lesson, a chore that he disliked intensely. Usually, he managed to palm it off to some of the younger women who had a musical bent, but the tightness of Elliot's curriculum had prevented that escape route. He had only a perfunctory knowledge of the mechanics of music, and no particular love for it, but he got by as best he could. On that day, he had been bored and restless, glad of any diversion, when he remembered reading somewhere that his new pupil had an aptitude for music and, with ill-disguised condescension, asked her if she would like to play for them. She hesitated, but he coaxed her with gentle sarcasm.

'I'm sure we'd all like to hear you play.'

She wasn't sure. The rest of the class fidgeted nervously, torn between a desire to hear her play, and a fear that their friend might be about to walk into some kind of trap. Then, her decision made, she handed her recorder to the safe-keeping of Susan Walker and opened the lid of the piano. He fetched a chair for her and instructed the class to sit on the floor. She stood at the yellowing keys for a second, then turned to face him.

'What would you like me to play, Mr Andrews?'

The class turned and looked at him with one face. Somehow, he felt his control of the situation slipping a little, and he responded defensively with more sarcasm.

'I'm sure, Lysandra, you have an extensive repertoire. Why don't you select any piece you consider appropriate?'

Turning back to the keys, she gently felt them with her fingers, as if practising the movements her hands would make, shuffled the chair closer to the piano and made herself comfortable. He went and stood at the back of the class where he could see everyone without them seeing him, and when she looked down at him, silently asking if she should start, he nodded his head. He had never heard the school piano played in such a way – it seemed different under her touch. Gone was the old, creaking heaviness that orchestrated each morning's assembly, and in its place danced a light-fingered richness of texture and tone that seemed to fill the hall and touch each of the listening children. It washed over them like sunlight and lit up the wooden floor, the faded curtains on the stage, the bamboo hoops and wooden benches, the wooden skittles standing listening in a silent corner. It slipped out an open window and circled the empty playground until the notes fragmented and dissolved in the rain. He stood and listened as the music washed over him, and for a second he closed his eyes against it. In the darkness of his memory, he saw a boy alone on a beach, skimming stones against the white-curled waves, watching the flat stone wing its way through the serried blackness. He felt again the cold smoothness of the stone in his hand and heard the

123

mocking calls of the watching gulls winging above his head. Then there was silence and in his ears he could hear nothing but rain beating against the windows of the hall. She had finished, and then, spontaneously, the class applauded, quietly at first, but increasingly louder, and he did nothing to stop it. Elliot's curious face appeared at a window, and then was gone. The applause ended and she slipped off the chair, embarrassment on her face, and went back into the relative anonymity of her place. He walked to the front of the class, and although he felt a strong obligation to say something, he was unsure of what it should be. He satisfied the needs of the situation with a brief and neutral statement of thanks, then reminded the class of the need to return to the classroom in absolute silence, but as he led the obedient procession, he could hear the music echoing inside his head with each step he took.

At times during the year their wills crossed, but only once did it have a serious aspect. He had been experiencing problems with his father and while he had anticipated a mental deterioration, the speed with which it came shocked him. His father slipped into disturbing periods when his mind wandered in some dark maze, lost in confusions and convoluted memories, and he frequently attempted to leave the house to visit people long dead, or streets the redeveloper's bulldozer had demolished. Restraining him proved difficult and energy-consuming, and the stress and frustrations involved in constant supervision began to wear him out. Then, despite efforts to prevent it, his father began to sleep during the day and at night awoke and attempted to dress himself. There was a growing danger of him stumbling about in the dark and falling down the stairs. His father also imagined strange and malevolent plots were being hatched by nameless conspirators, asserting that the house was about to be taken over and all their possessions sold; that Mrs Mitchell was in league with them and the police should be informed before it was too late.

While he tried hard not to let his problems at home affect his work, there were days when he found himself on edge and irritated by trivial and irrelevant issues that normally he would have handled with ease. With his concentration divided between home and school, he put less into his teaching and got less out of it. One morning, when Elliot was attending a course, he found himself burdened with additional administrative responsibilities that necessitated visits to the school office. It was when he was returning from one of these that he was met at the end of the corridor by a storm of noise, and he could feel his anger and frustration rising closer and closer to the surface. Could he not leave them for five minutes without chaos ensuing? It was naive to think that children would work as silently or as diligently in his absence, whatever instructions or threats might be left looming over their heads, but the riot that he could hear was more than he had previously considered possible. It goaded him momentarily with the thought that his control was shallow and transient, and as he walked quickly but quietly, he was determined to give no indication of his imminent arrival. As he approached the rear of the classroom he could detect singing, and, stopping at the window, he peered over the frosted glass. The Lawrenson girl was conducting the class, a wooden ruler substituting as a baton, and Thomas Montgomery, a gullible dunderhead of a boy, was standing out at the front being serenaded – it was his birthday and they were celebrating it in song. Suddenly, someone detected his presence, and, like a creature scenting danger, Montgomery bolted to the safety of his desk, while immediate and total silence snapped shut over the class. Heads dropped to books and not a shoe scuffed the frozen air or a page of paper rustled the stillness as he entered the room. He entered slowly, almost as if nothing was wrong, but his deliberate and weighted steps carried the menace of impending eruption.

'How dare you make such a racket! Put your pens down – there's no point in pretending to work now! I could hear that noise at the end of the corridor and every other class in the school could, too. Can I not leave you for five minutes? Can I not leave you for five single minutes without coming back to this?'

His voice vibrated with genuine anger and he felt his self-control ebbing away. He smashed his fist down on the front desk, making books and pens bounce and its occupier jerk back into the seat with fear.

'You know I won't have this! You know I won't tolerate this sort of behaviour in any class of mine.'

His eyes raked the room, almost wishing to see a challenging look of defiance, or indifference, but there was none to vent his risen fury on.

'You'll all stay in at break time and you'll not speak for the rest of this day – not a word will I hear in this room!'

But it was not enough, and his unappeased anger sought a victim.

'Thomas Montgomery – come out to the front.'

The boy scrambled to the front like a summoned dog, and as he stood in the vast solitude, his body trembled with expectancy. Without taking his eyes off the boy, he went to the cupboard and found the cane it had not been necessary to use for a long time. Wordlessly, he signalled the boy towards him.

'Put out your hand and don't let me ever catch you out of your seat again without permission so long as you're a pupil of this school.'

The boy held out his hand in a quivering silence while his upper teeth bit hard on his lower lip and his other hand clenched the side of his ill-fitting shorts. Adjusting the level of the boy's hand, he raised the bamboo cane in the air, as the boy flinched and screwed his eyes tightly shut in anticipation.

'Please, Mr Andrews, we were all making noise . . . it was because it was his birthday and we wanted to . . . '

The cane froze. He knew where the voice came from without turning to look, and he struggled to resist a pounding desire to smash her into submission. He longed to hurt her.

'Don't dare speak unless you're asked to! When I want your comments, Lysandra Lawrenson, I'll ask you for them.'

The cane fell with a whistle of wind and the boy's hand jerked convulsively. Then the other hand. Then, deliberately looking in her direction, he raised the cane again and cut him a third time. The boy stifled a squeal, then wrung his lacerated hands as if trying to wash away the pain. Blinking back the tears, he lumbered back to his desk and grasped the cold comfort of the desk's metal stanchions.

It was over now, and as his anger subsided, he felt ashamed that he had let his self-control slip in such a public way, but he showed no sign of regret or remorse to the class, nor was there any going back on his declared punishment. The day dragged on, irredeemably miserable, and as if afraid of what he might see, he avoided meeting her gaze or making any kind of contact. But despite this physical avoidance he still thought about her – something he was increasingly aware of doing – and he knew now that she would hate him like all the others. He told himself it made no difference; he told himself it was for the best, but he had a vague feeling of loss, of some undefined door being slowly closed.

One day, some time later, when he was doing lunch duty, he paused at the window overlooking the playground. Down below, the clusters of children concentrated instinctively on their play, temporarily released from the restrictions of the classroom and oblivious to his scrutiny. As always, his eyes picked her out, even in the middle of a large group. They were getting ready to play some game, and she was selecting teams as all the children stood in a circle with one foot pointing inwards. She was tapping each foot lightly and although he could not hear, he knew they were chanting some rhyme. He watched the blackness of her hair bobbing in rhythm and when she had finished, half the circle broke away and fled in all directions. It was a game of chain tig. He watched her join hands with Mary Blair, and as they took off in pursuit, he was struck by how mis-matched they were. Compared with the heavy, clumsy Mary Blair, the child looked like a sprite. As he watched the pattern of the game evolving, his eyes always returned to the same pair. Then, while running at speed in a desperate effort to catch their quarry, the heavier girl pulled too strongly and, suddenly, caused her partner to stumble and sprawl on the ground. She looked hurt, and with real concern, he hurried to the playground. As he did so, he resolved to ban such dangerous games and reprimanded himself for his laxity in not having foreseen such an outcome.

When he arrived, helping hands were already picking the girl up and guiding her towards the door of the school. He took immediate control of the situation and made a careful assessment of the injury, realising with some relief that although she had two badly cut knees and a skinned palm where she had tried to break her fall, nothing was broken. She was trying to be brave, but the tears were beginning to well up in her eyes, and without knowing why, he didn't want the rest of the class to see her crying, so he ushered her quickly into an empty room. He allowed Ann Brown to accompany them, in the hope that her presence might be a comfort. There was grit in the cuts, and from one a steady trickle of blood was reddening the top of her white sock. Taking out a handkerchief, he gently pressed it to her knee. He dispatched Ann Brown to the office for first-aid materials, and as he knelt down on the floor dabbing her red and skinned knees, he felt awkward and nervous. She was crying a little, but battling to hold it back, and running out of things to say, he silently urged the messenger to hurry up. He got her to roll her socks down, and as she did so, he noticed that one of her red shoes was scuffed and scratched. Ann Brown returned, and with a swab of cotton wool and antiseptic, he cleaned the cuts. She winced with pain as it stung and smarted, and he felt her hand gripping his shoulder, the smallness of the hand belying the tightness of the grip. With the experience gained from many similar ministrations, he finished the first-aid and then phoned for her mother to come and collect her. By that time, however, she had made a good recovery, and if her mother had permitted it, would have stayed in school. In the coming months she wore the scabs on her knees like badges of honour.

Three days later, a messenger came to his room and told him there was a phone call for him. As he walked quickly to the school office, he knew that it was a call from home, and his mind raced through the possibilities. It was worse than he had feared. Mrs Mitchell told him that his father had collapsed and the family doctor had called an ambulance to take him to hospital. He could tell from her voice as she was giving him details that she was badly shaken, and he tried as best he could to calm her and get as many facts as possible. Elliot covered his class and he went straight to the hospital, where a doctor who seemed disconcertingly young told him his father had suffered a stroke and offered him a patronising sympathy. The condescension masked a marked reluctance to commit himself to any specific prediction about his father's chances or future disability. There was nothing to do but wait. He was not allowed to see his father, and after several hours was advised to go home.

He did not go home directly, but drove aimlessly round the city, the mechanical control of the car soothing and steadying his nerves. He felt curiously calm, almost as if the worst had happened and the moment had passed. Eventually, he headed for home, stopping on the way to thank Mrs Mitchell for her assistance and because she had asked him to let her know how his father was. By the time he arrived home, it was quite late. The house was in darkness and as he put the key in the lock, the familiar act seemed strange and somehow different. He pushed the door open and stood for a moment on the doorstep, staring into the silent shadows of the hall, as greyness filtered through the banisters and ebbed through the open doorways. The house hovered above him, holding itself deadly and still, and he hesitated to enter. His hand instinctively found the light switch, but he did not turn it on. He paused again to let his eyes adjust to the gloom, then closed the door behind him. Voices whispered to him from the darkness of corners and long-forgotten memories murmured from the breathing, rustling stillness as each step echoed in the empty shell that cupped itself over his soul. The tick of a clock drummed to the beat of his heart and the hall mirror broke its uneasy sleep to reflect his passing in a blink of grey. He walked through the downstairs rooms, touching familiar furniture for reassurance, until he reached the open door of the sitting room. Something led him forward despite his fear. A yellow street lamp tinged the room. Sitting on a chair, he looked about with the curiosity of a man remembering the past; at his mother's china teasets entombed in the glass-fronted cabinet; framed photographs frozen under the weight of glass; brass ornaments grown dull and cold. His eyes rested on what he knew was a photograph of himself as a young man, lingering only long enough to taste the bitterness of wasted years. He sank back into the chair and wondered where the years had gone, then pulled his coat tighter about him as a passing car's headlights shone into the greyness. For the second time, he saw a young boy on a beach, and in his ears he heard the incessant thunder of the angry waves as they broke upon the shore of his loneliness. Then, his thoughts turned back to his father and he resolved to ring the hospital and enquire about his condition. His eyes rested momentarily on the piano that stood dark and heavy, trapped eternally in its own silence, and he heard again the music of the school piano. He thought, too, of her, and he found comfort in his thoughts, and then, as always, he remembered the way she looked at him and the undefined emotion he saw in her eyes.

For four days there was no sign of change in his father's condition, but he was very ill, and his chances of recovery hung in the balance. He visited the hospital twice each day, once in the afternoon, when Elliot covered his class and let him slip away half an hour before the end of school, and once in the evening. His father lay in a semi-conscious state, unable to speak. When his eyes did open, they communicated no acknowledgment or recognition. He was in a room of his own and there was no restriction on the visiting time. The minutes dragged by, and as he sat at the bedside he searched his father's hollow face for some spark of life or familiar expression, but there was none to be found. Then, self-consciously at first, he began to talk, in the hope that his words might evoke some response. His voice sounded faltering and uncertain in the stillness, different from the one he heard each day in his classroom, but gradually it took courage and stepped diffidently into the silence. He talked about anything that came into his head – the weather, the garden, events in school, things he had read in the newspaper, about himself.

'I know you think about the past a lot. I've been thinking about it too. There's something keeps coming back to me, it comes back clearly all these years later as if it was yesterday, and I can't get it out of my head. It's that first holiday – do you remember it, dad? I was about eight years old and you'd rented that old ramshackle house that backed on to the beach – the one with the bed bugs and an outside toilet that I wouldn't use for the first couple of days. Do you remember that beach? I must've lived on it for the whole two weeks. It's what comes back to me now – that wide stretch of sand, with its stinking wrack of seaweed and shells shining among the shingle like coloured glass. Standing there and skimming stones, standing there and suddenly feeling very small and frightened. Frightened by the sea, by its depth and size, frightened by the waves breaking and breaking and never ceasing. Frightened that it might snatch me off the shore and drown me in its deepest, darkest depths. I feel frightened now, dad. All these years later, and it's come back.'

He paused while outside in the corridor some kind of trolley rattled by. Voices in his head urged him to stop, but as his tongue savoured the unaccustomed sweetness of freedom, he brushed them recklessly aside.

'There's a new girl in my class. Her name is Lysandra. I've never told you about her, have I? I wanted to talk about her many times, but I stopped myself. She's a strange girl – not like any of the rest – with a mind of her own and very clever. Sometimes there's no telling her, and when she does art, half the time she makes up her own measurements. Dad, can you hear me? Her name is Lysandra and she can play the piano better than any child I've ever heard. Sometimes, I imagine she'll come to the house and play our piano for us. That'd be something, dad, wouldn't it? Maybe when you're better she'll come, maybe when you're better we'll start having a few visitors about the place, try to get out of the rut we've got ourselves stuck in. What about it, dad? What do you say? And she's not frightened of me – sometimes she looks at me and I'm not sure what it is she's thinking. When I notice her looking at me I feel . . . '

He froze in embarrassed silence as a nurse came into the room to check his father. She offered him a cup of tea, but he mumbled a refusal and told her he was just about to go. He waited until she had gone, then stood up and buttoned up his overcoat against the rain that was falling outside. Neither his father's expression nor position had changed during the visit. Bending over the bed, he touched his father gently on the shoulder, then turned up the collar of his coat and made his way out into the darkness and the rain.

His father died two days later. Although he had been preparing himself for it, the actual moment still came as a shock, but he felt no rush of grief, only a kind of numbness, a vague nothingness that seeped through his whole being. He searched inwardly for the appropriate emotion, but could not deceive himself, and as a substitute, busied himself with the necessary arrangements and formalities. Visitors called to offer sympathy – an unpleasant embarrassment for all parties. He wished he had inserted a 'house strictly private' line in the newspaper death notice. Mrs Mitchell arrived early one morning with two tins of buns she had baked, because she knew he would need to provide hospitality for his visitors. He thanked her sincerely, and he could see that she was genuinely upset by his father's death. He had always assumed that his father had merely represented a difficult and unco-operative charge, and it surprised him to realise that some kind of relationship had existed between the two. When everything was over, and all his father's affairs were settled, he resolved to make her a final payment in respect of her faithful patience. Then it struck him that she would not be coming to the house again, and he thought of asking if she would like to pick something to take with her as a keepsake, but he did not know how to put it to her, and, fearful that she might be offended, he let the moment pass. He watched her put on the headscarf with its pictures of Paris, and, walking her to the gate, stood watching as she hurried out of his life.

There were not many people at the funeral, just a few dutiful family representatives, some people he recognised from his mother's former connection with the local church, and a sprink-ling of casual friends and acquaintances. Elliot was there, blandly sympathetic and irritating with his trite reassurances. Worse than that was the fact that he had brought six pupils from his class. What had the man been thinking of? He felt angry and disturbed, but it was too late to do or say anything about this intrusion into his personal life, and he would not look near them nor meet their curious stares. Standing at the graveside with their eyes fixed on him, he felt disturbingly defenceless, almost naked before them, and he longed for the barren ritual to be over. But to his annoyance, the minister, with his audience's minds focused una-voidably on eternity, preached at length and eventually he let his eyes wander round the faces of the assembled group. To one side stood Elliot with the children grouped about him, and as he looked at them, they averted their eyes as if caught in a guilty act. Only one face met his. He looked into her eyes and saw again the emotion that he had come to recognise, but could put no name to. She stared at him and in that moment he knew that what he saw, and had always seen, was pity. Only the strength of his will held him to the spot as the world blurred before his sight, and the minister's closing words faded into oblivion. People were shaking his hand and he mumbled incoherencies in response as he searched in his pockets for the envelopes that con-tained the money for the gravediggers, and for a moment was unable to find them. The minister was making some excuse about having to hurry to his next engagement, while he scraped the sole of his shoe over an edging stone to free it from the mud that had caked to it. People were moving away in little knots of twos and threes, and the gravediggers impatiently handled their spades in readiness, but he stood motionless, watching as the mourners walked briskly in the direction of their cars. Then sud-denly, and without his being aware of her route of approach, she was standing before him. Her face was pinched with the cold, and wisps of black hair flicked in the breeze. She pushed them away from her eyes with her hand, and stood looking at him, and for a moment neither of them spoke. When she did, her voice was quick and nervous.

'I'm very sorry about your father. I hope you'll be back to teach us soon.'

Then she turned away and began to walk towards where Elliot was shepherding the other children into his car.

He called after her, his voice sounding weak and wavering.

'Lysandra!'

She stopped and turned to face him again. He hesitated, then held out his hand towards her.

'Thank you for coming.'

For a second, he held the small warmth of her hand in his, and then she, too, was gone. He watched as she started to run towards the waiting Elliot.

He was alone now, and pulling his coat tightly about him for strength, he looked deliberately into the grave for the last time. Finding composure at last, he stepped off the wooden boards and walked quickly and steadily towards the funeral car. As he did so he could hear the spades of the gravediggers shovelling the sodden clay on to his father's coffin.

The heavy wooden pencil case clattered to the floor, shattering the dream of silence that had settled lightly on the room. Its noise was terrible to him, splintering the soft web of memory he had woven and letting the present wash coldly over him once more. Pencils rolled thunderously across the floor, until trapped by the legs of chairs and desks. Their owner frantically scrambled after the contents, banging her head on the bottom of a desk in her desperate haste to restore the calm she had so carelessly disturbed. The sound of the pencils rattling back into the box speared his soul, and his whole being urged her to be still, but he could not bring himself to speak. About the room heads lifted, glad of the momentary distraction from their work, and watched the embarrassed girl take her seat again, then sheepishly reorganise the objects on her desk. A restless quiet surfaced again, but feet shuffled and chairs creaked. He knew it was time to inspect their work, time to punish Thomas Murray, but he could find no strength to do either. From the back wall, the red flowers burned so brightly that his eyes could not bear the fierce intensity of their flame. He gripped the sides of his desk, but felt only her hand on his shoulder, saw again her red shoes with their scuffed and scratched leather. And then, in an older memory, he heard his feet scrunching the gravelly shingle that beaded the beach, felt his fingers picking out precious stones that glistened with jewelled dampness – finding a smooth, flat stone and skimming the waves, skipping through their curled crests like a winged dolphin. A chair scraped across the floor. Someone coughed. He knew it was nearly time. Suddenly, the sky blackened and arched over him like a great predatory bird hovering in readiness, its yellow stalking eyes the only stars. The laughing sea darkened and deepened, and each wave that broke called gently to him, whispering his name, calling him home. Somewhere far off, he could hear a bell slowly ringing. Impatience began to ripple through the room. He sat on, motionless and silent, oblivious to everything, feeling only the waves washing slowly and relentlessly over him.

LOUISE

LOUISE FOUND the mirror unkind. During the course of any day she spoke to it many times, but when she listened to what it had to say, it never told her what she wanted to hear. Louise never fully believed what she heard and so she would often slide back before it in the hope that it might tell her something new. When her hopes were unrealised, her spirit was not crushed, but suffered only a little twist of disappointment. She knew the mirror did not really wish to be unkind and she knew, too, that there was always tomorrow. Sometimes when she walked by it, and knew it was not really thinking of her, she would glance secretly at it in the hope of capturing the truth by stealth.

The mirror told her that her nose was too short and stubby, her eyes were closer to a grey colour when they should have been green, and that she had too many freckles. She saw red hair that was short and waveless, and bristling with an anarchy that defied the most ruthless brush. Her face was open and devoid of mystery. In her heart she believed truly that the face the mirror showed her every day was not her own. It could not be. The spirit that fountained and dolphined inside her could not be matched with such a face. Someone, perhaps, had taken hers by mistake, and left this one in its place. She wondered what her real face looked like. Sometimes in a magazine she saw a beautiful woman and wondered if she might be the thief. She squinted at the mirror and tried to believe that time would bring her beauty. There were moments when she felt so beautiful inside that she was sure it must seep through her skin and be visible for all to see. Now her thirteenth birthday was approaching, she looked at it more often and a kind of desperation grew in her looking.

As the date approached, she became quiet and preoccupied, so absorbed in her own thoughts and feelings that her parents' suggestion came as a complete surprise. She was delighted. It was the most exciting birthday treat that any girl could wish for, a colourful prospect that promised her thirteenth birthday would be a complete success. The very word 'circus' conjured up a vision of sparkling spectacle and magic moments that was more attractive than any party. Although she had never admitted it to anyone, her last birthday party had not been a success. The boys had been bored and restless and spoilt many of the games with their rowdiness. They had not mixed well with the girls, preferring to tease them and engage in competitive roughness. As for the girls, they had divided into tight friendship groups and made little effort to mix. At times, Louise felt she was not quite the centre of attraction that a birthday girl might be entitled to expect. The party had eventually petered into nothing and despite her cheerful public face she had been disappointed and a little hurt. Even the sum total of her presents had not amounted to much – small, impersonal, functional items that did little to cheer her failing spirits. A birthday should be special, one of the most special days of the year. And so Louise received the news that she and her younger sister were to be taken to the circus with relief. Although she suspected that her parents had conceived the idea to avoid a party, it did nothing to diminish its appeal.

As the day grew nearer, Louise found herself looking more closely at the mirror. She knew what she hoped to see, but could find no trace of it, searching with an intensity of desire that gave her pain. She sought no dramatic transformation but would have been satisfied with even the slightest indication of change, some small step on the mysterious path that led to beauty. But no matter how often she looked, the mirror did not tell her what she wanted to hear, and she began to hate it. She brushed her rebellious red hair until her arms were sore and saw no difference from when she had started. Her grey-not-green eyes stared hungrily into its depths and turned away empty and unsatisfied. But there was still time.

One afternoon when her parents had gone shopping she was

left to look after Frances. Leaving her younger sister watching television cartoons she slipped into her mother's bedroom. Sitting at the dressing table she gently touched the jars and bottles, delicately opening lids and closing them again after smelling the contents. The bottles and containers were themselves attractive, and she fingered each one with pleasure before making sure she returned it to its exact position on the dresser. She sprayed perfume lightly on her wrist and sniffed the fragrant scent. Then she began to apply make-up in the ritual sequence that she had watched her mother follow so many times. Thickly spread foundation cream camouflaged the stippling of freckles and blusher fanned her cheeks into flame. With her mouth round and open in concentration, she applied mascara slowly and precisely, then painted her eyelids pearly peach. The mirror told her that everything was wrong, but like someone painting a picture, she persevered in the hope that the final stroke might make everything right. Then with a final flourish she pursed her lips and coloured them deepest red.

'You look like a clown, Louie.'

The lipstick clattered on to the dresser, fragmenting the trance she had drifted into. Spinning round, she saw her young sister standing in the doorway of the bedroom, one hand clutching a crumpled bag of crisps and the other a favourite blanket.

'You look funny, Louie. What you got on your face?'

Like a thief caught with her hand in a pocket, Louise felt a shock of panic. In her rush for an escape she paused for neither subtlety nor guile.

'If you tell mummy, I won't take you with me to the circus.'

Frances stared into her sister's angry grey eyes with the peach-coloured lids and her fiery mouth, and was frightened into silence. Tears welled in her eyes.

'I won't tell, Louie. I won't tell. Promise.'

The look of fear on her sister's face stabbed Louise with remorse. She crouched down and rested her hands on the child's shoulders.

'It's all right, Frances – I didn't mean it. Everything's all right. The circus will be really good, won't it? It'll be really good. Just keep this a secret – our secret. Now go back down and watch television and I'll be down in a minute.'

Trailing her blanket, Frances left the room, a little sprinkling of crisps from the burst bag flaking in her wake. Grabbing a handful of tissues, Louise scoured her face clean, then went to the bathroom and washed and scrubbed till there was no trace of make-up.

A week before her birthday, Louise was taken by her mother and with her guidance was allowed to pick a new dress. They went on a Saturday afternoon and the shops were crowded and unhelpful. At first the trip was a frustrating failure as their initial enthusiasm dissolved into a pessimistic trudge. Eventually, however, they found a dress that they both liked and which fitted perfectly. After its purchase they went into a coffee shop and Louise felt a firm flush of adulthood. Opposite their table sat two girls in their late teens who were very pretty and wore elegantly fashionable clothes. She watched them with a deep fascination that distracted her from the fragile cake she was too nervous to eat. She envied their effortless good looks and wondered what they had been like as children. Surely it could not be just a question of pure luck – if it was, then life was cruel and unfair to reward some and reject others. She knew she was not ugly but she knew, too, that she did not see in the mirror what she wanted to see. It was not that she wanted to be uniquely, head-turningly beautiful, but she did desire, more than anything else in the world, to possess the face that was truly hers. What her true face looked like, she wasn't sure, but she believed in her heart that some day she would find it, a belief born not out of optimism, but grounded in an eternal conviction of the inevitable triumph of truth.

When she returned home, she tried on her dress in the privacy of her own room. The mirror told her that it was pretty and expensive, but that the overall effect was not quite right. She looked and looked, but could not put a name to what was wrong. Brushing her hair with passion, she pulled it back from her face in a variety of styles, but it resisted stubbornly any suppression of its unbridled freedom. Balancing precariously in a pair of her mother's high heels, she tottered unsteadily about the room. Suddenly, she heard her sister bunny-hopping up the stairs and, turning too sharply, tripped over herself and sprawled on the floor. In fear of creases and fluff, she scrambled to her feet just in time to hear Frances close the bathroom door behind her. She sat on the bed and felt foolish and just a little afraid. Time was growing short.

They parked in sight of the tent. Frances wanted to run ahead but her mother restrained her enthusiasm with a sharp word. Louise welcomed the imposition of dignity on her younger sister – this was her treat and she wanted nothing to detract from it. They joined a long queue of other families and she felt comfortingly secure between her parents. Brightly coloured clowns appeared, working their way down the line, selling programmes and joking with children. One of the clowns was on huge stilts. He towered over the queue and seemed like a giant to Louise. Each time he took a step, she bit her lip at the thought of him losing his balance and tumbling to the distant earth in a mixture of broken wood and bone. However, her fear soon turned to laughter as he spread his rigid legs and the clowns ran between them. It was a tantalising preview of what was to come.

In a few minutes they were seated in the big tent. Frances seemed unimpressed as she sat on the wooden bench.

'It smells funny, mummy. It smells not nice.'

The child voiced what Louise was thinking, but she was irritated by her younger sister's constant craving to draw attention to herself. Louise felt that she was intruding into the spotlight reserved for her. The irritation soon passed. It was the animals she liked best. The tigers looked so fierce and frightening. They paraded around the ring in a stealthy prowl which combined pride and disdain. They seemed insulted by the paucity of the tricks they were asked to do, and yet she felt that beneath their bored exteriors burned a savage power. Somehow, the bars of the ring did not look strong enough to hold them if they chose to burst through. She snuggled up to her father for security.

The lion tamer cracked his whip and snarled at the big cats with heroic bravado. Occasionally, one of the lions would turn on him and paw the air belligerently and then he responded vigorously by imposing his will on the defiant beast, confronting it with commanding gestures and movements. And yet all the time he conveyed a very real sense of danger and vulnerability. Louise admired his courage and thought he looked very handsome. He wore a black shirt and black trousers with a red braid down the leg. His hair was very black and shiny and his skin was brown and suntanned. He smiled a gleaming, white smile, and he used his face and eyes to show all the different emotions he was experiencing. Louise thought he was very brave and gave little squeals of fear whenever a lion seemed to threaten him, clapping enthusiastically when he bowed elaborately after each successful trick. As in all the acts, she felt he was performing just for her, in honour of her birthday, and she was swept along on a wave of excitement. Suddenly, two lions seemed to unite in gestures of aggressive defiance, pawing the air and snarling angrily. Jumping forward, the lion tamer cracked his whip at the delinquent creatures, snapping it about their heads with sharp flicks of his wrist. Enraged, the animals reared up rebelliously. The crowd rustled with concern and Louise gave a cry of horror, but the danger passed almost as quickly as it had come. Standing on his tiptoes and holding his whip like a matador's sword, he hung over the beasts until they cowered like domestic cats. The applause reached a crescendo.

Three brightly coloured clowns bounced and rolled into the ring, their outsized suits a blazing patchwork of gaudy colours. Red-nosed, white-faced and small-hatted, they clowned their way through a riot of cars that fell apart, buckets of water, pies in the face, tumbles and trips. Their crazy antics made her laugh openly and with some surprise she heard her laughter mingle with that of her mother and father. Then suddenly one of the clowns was chasing another to where they were sitting. At the last second the intended victim ducked and immediately every-one around her did the same as a full bucket of water headed in their direction, but to a roar of laughter, they were covered in nothing more than a spray of confetti. While they were still shaking the tiny pieces of paper out of their hair, there was a dramatic fanfare and a troupe of white horses cantered into the ring.

With the horses came the most beautiful girl Louise had ever seen. Her hair was jet black and tied in a sleek ponytail with a pink ribbon. Her brown eyes flashed and sparkled like diamonds. The horses, too, were beautiful. They were completely white and pranced lightly round the ring, resplendent in their blue sequined saddle cloths and red plumes. The horses cantered and trotted in synchronised rhythm and wove a tracery of intricate patterns around the sawdust ring. The girl had a little stringed whip, but it was used only to direct and point, and was without menace. At a command, the horses faced inwards in a circle and rose up on their hind legs. Louise watched her reward them with pats and slaps. The horses seemed to love her and she, in turn, to love them. In the climax of her act she balanced on the back of one of the horses and performed graceful balances and pirouettes as the horses galloped round in a kaleidoscope of hooves and coloured plumes.

Then, suddenly, in an inexplicable moment of knowledge, Louise knew that she had seen her face. She was sure, and she was sure that, having found it, she would somehow, somewhere, share in its beauty. Her soul rode wild and free on the pure white horses and happiness broke inside her like a wave. She wanted to tell someone but there was no one to listen and even if there had been, she did not know the words to use. It seemed as if on this, her thirteenth birthday, fate had brought her to this moment and this truth. The blue sequins sparkled and the white horses circled in a rhythmic dance that spun her soul round and round with exultant excitement. Everything else faded into oblivion at the matchless richness of this birthday gift. It was gold, frankincense and myrrh – it was her most precious of gifts. Louise watched transfixed as the white horses rounded the ring for the final time and then vanished.

After this moment all the other acts blended into a blur. Acrobats and jugglers, strong-men and tightrope walkers paraded for her delight and she enjoyed them all, but nothing could break the spell of the white horses and the girl who had shown her her true face. When her father asked if she was enjoying herself she could not bring herself to trust her voice and replied by smiling and snuggling even closer to him. Frances, too, was engrossed by it all, only breaking her attention long enough to consume a pink cloud of candy floss, some of which stuck to her face and hands. Louise smiled at her and felt affection for her. She was glad her sister had shared her birthday treat.

Gradually, the evening wore on and the remaining acts paled in comparison with what she had seen. She hoped in vain for some kind of grand finale where the girl and her white horses might reappear, but there was no indication that this might happen. She grew impatient and frustrated, and when the clowns reappeared, she found it hard to hide her disappointment. Their loud slapstick grew tiresome and she could not bring herself to laugh. Only one impulse was in her heart now, and the desire to see the face again grew stronger by the second. It grew until it became a hunger that had to be satisfied. Whispering an untruth to her mother and gently rebuffing any offer of company, she slipped quietly out of the row of seats and down the wooden-tiered aisle. Where exactly she was going she did not know, but she felt irresistibly drawn to find the face she wanted for her own.

Her hands plucked nervously at her party dress as she picked her way through a maze of caravans and trailers. Behind her, she could hear the applause of the crowd; in front she was vaguely aware of voices shouting but the words were lost in the noise. Everything was bathed in a strange yellow light that distorted shapes into twisted shadows. Meeting a passing circus hand, she stepped out with greater purpose in an attempt to convince him of her right to be there, but he seemed oblivious to her presence and preoccupied with the costumes he was carrying. She threaded her way through circus debris, skirting wooden crates and trailers. The sound of voices grew louder. Breaking into a floodlit clearing she reached the source. At the rear of an open horsebox sat a man she recognised as the lion tamer. Beside the box white horses were tethered in a line. Stripped of their glittering saddle cloths and plumes, they huddled together for warmth. Their grey tails hung lifelessly and flecks of sweat lathered their bodies and dropped on to the festering sprinkling of straw. As she approached, a shiver rippled through the line and they shuffled their feet restlessly. Their owner stood facing the man lounging arrogantly on the open trailer. His shirt was open to the waist and he drank from a large green bottle, taking deep slugs and wiping his mouth with the back of a hand. Louise drew back into the shadows and watched.

She was close enough to see the face she was seeking. The thick, cracked layer of make-up was bleached white by the cruel light and dark pools of mascara smouldered under the eyes. The no longer young face was ravaged by a bitter spasm of hate as her eyes slit into black knives that burned to lacerate the man in front of her.

'You said that slut meant nothing to you!' she screamed, her voice wild and piercing. 'You said you'd done with her.'

'I've told you a thousand times, it's all over. Why can't you believe it? Just once in your miserable drunken life, why can't you believe the truth when you hear it?'

There was a second of silence and then, like some wounded beast, the woman hurled herself against her tormentor with a howl of rage and pain. Louise pulled further back into the shadows. Standing up, the man repulsed the frenzied attack and then, with one arm, contemptuously flung his attacker to the ground. She lay on the filthy straw, sobbing and breathlessly firing curses into the air. Then suddenly, amid the diatribe, something touched a raw nerve, and as Louise stood trembling in the darkness, she watched the man leap down to the side of the horsebox. In a flashing green arc the bottle smashed against the metal side and showered green diamonds of light. The line of horses jerked and whimpered with fear.

'Say another word and I'll cut the throat of one of your precious animals. Say one more word and I'll slash it from ear to ear!'

And as he spoke, he brandished the jagged bottle in the air.

Stumbling and almost falling, Louise ran as fast as she could, neither knowing nor caring in which direction she was heading. Hot, stinging tears welled up in her eyes and struggled to be released. She ran and ran, splashes of mud spotting her legs and dress. Her chest was tight with pain and her breath came in deep, heaving gasps. Still she ran. Above her, the sky tented in sequined blackness and from behind her burst a great crescendo of laughter. The clowns were performing. She felt ringed in an unbreakable circle of bitterness. New tears of anguish filled her eyes, for in her heart she knew they were laughing at her.

THE FISHING TRIP

THE BOAT headed steadily out to sea. It dipped and rose gently through the swelling waves with a firm sense of direction that reassured him. In front of them stretched an empty expanse of distance that spread to the horizon; behind, the diminishing security of a familiar shore. He stood watching the white wake unwind itself easily and wondered where they were heading. The lighthouse blinked light and gulls wheeled effortlessly above, their cries drowned by the remorseless chug of the boat's engine. His father stood hunched in the tiny entrance of the wheelhouse, holding his large frame steady with one outstretched arm. He could hear him laughing with the skipper, but all the other noises mingled to smother their words. It was strange to see his father so relaxed and at his ease among his men, men who were known to him only as a result of his father's passing references. It was strange, too, how wrong the impressions he had formed had been. None of the men resembled in any way his mental picture of them. A little salted spray splashed his face. He wished he could hear what his father was laughing at.

Gradually, the sea was growing rougher, and soon the shore seemed a long way off. There was no going back now. A few of the men began to bait and feather their lines. He watched them curiously. Out of uniform and away from the world of duty they looked as excited as schoolboys. Their jokes and banter seemed curiously similar to what he heard every day in school, as they flourished flamboyantly coloured feathers in a competitive parody of expertise. Some of them offered to help him, and he was pleased by the way they didn't patronise him or show any obvious deference because of his father's rank, and he accepted

147

their help gladly, making a little joke of his inexperience. They seemed to accept him naturally as one of their own. It was strange for him to see how they related to his father – it was almost as if he was a different man from the one he knew. This newness intrigued him and swirled around his head as the growing swell bucked the boat.

His father's invitation to join the fishing party had surprised him. Now that he was seventeen, their leisure time activities rarely coincided. He had almost refused out of habit, assuming that any adult expedition would be boring. His father had seemed a little embarrassed when he had invited him, almost suggesting reasons for why his son might not want to go. Why he had actually accepted was not clear in his own mind, but he was glad that he had chosen to go. He felt surprisingly at ease among these men who served with his father. What they were like as people when they wore uniform he did not know, but as a team of men on a summer's evening fishing trip, they were strangely childish and uninhibited in their pursuit of a temporary freedom. His father amazed him – he was like leader of the gang, shouting out a gibberish of nautical commands and advice that was markedly at odds with the quiet sobriety that characterised his usual speech and manner. The men responded with mock salutes and hearty 'aye, aye, captain's as if leading seamen in some pirate crew. There were many in-jokes and comic references to people and events he didn't understand, but he found himself laughing all the same, and his laughter somehow made him feel part of them. A hip flask was produced and passed around, discreetly avoiding him as it moved about the boat. With some curiosity, he wondered if his father would take a swig – he had never seen him drink before – but he was never to know the answer as his father had vanished inside the wheelhouse. Realising that he had lost eye contact sent a momentary shiver of insecurity through him, echoing a childish feeling he had long forgotten. He laughed inwardly at himself and turned his face to the sea.

A few minutes later his thoughts were disturbed by some activity at the rear of the boat. There was a burst of stifled laughter and frantic movements, the purpose of which he couldn't follow. Then suddenly, like misbehaving schoolboys who hear the approach of the returning teacher, everyone involved sprang back to his original position. Bemused and intrigued, he watched their intended victim return to where his fishing rod was propped against the side of the boat. As he noticed that the line was dangling over the side, a voice shouted,

'Hey, George, come quick – you've caught something!'

All the men cheered, and shouted encouragement and ludicrous advice as George, a portly, good-humoured man, began sceptically to wind in his line. He joined them as they began to hum with exaggerated drama the music from *Jaws*. As George, playing to the gallery, swung the fish aboard, there was a volley of cheers which changed to uproarious laughter as he unhooked an obviously rubber fish. As soon as he did this, one of the men grabbed it and began to hammer it with a wooden mallet. It bounced and skimmed across the deck, ricocheting against the circle of spectators. He watched from its edge but shared in the joke, feeling slightly relieved that someone else had been the victim. George seemed to take it all in good spirit and the episode was closed when he rescued his catch and announced,

'Sure with a bit of sauce it'll not taste any worse than the rest of the wife's cooking!'

After this excitement there was a temporary lull. As the boat continued its dogged path, he watched the flanking gulls and wondered at their stamina and effortless aerobatics.

'How's it going, then?'

Turning sharply round, he realised that his father had sidled up the boat and now stood at his shoulder.

'Not so bad. I don't know, though, if I'll catch anything.'

'Don't worry about that – if this lot can catch fish anyone can. Before the night's out they'll be jumping on to your hook.'

His father rested his arms on the edge of the boat and stared out at the sea. There was a moment's silence between them. Made uncomfortable by it, he searched for a reply.

'Are the men always like this?' he asked.

His father laughed and, turning round, surveyed the crew.

'Only in their own time. When they're working, they're a good team – I've never worked with any better. Don't let them fool you – it's just a healthy way to let off steam. Some of them have gone through some rough times, seen things they'll never be able to forget, no matter how hard they try.'

His father fumbled with some hooks then looked out to sea again.

'How's school going?'

'Okay, I suppose. It took a while to get used to it. It's a lot different from the last one.'

'I know it hasn't helped having to move so often. I hope it hasn't messed things up for you. If it's any consolation, I think this move will be the last for some time – it looks like I've got on as far as I'm going to for a good while yet.'

'Is getting on difficult, then?'

'Hard enough, I suppose. It's all a question of pretending to be an expert to some people and a know-nothing to others. Being in the right place at the right time helps too, of course.'

There was silence again. He was vaguely conscious of never having talked with his father in this way before. A gull swooped low and parallel with the boat. Then he felt a soft wordless pat on his back and turned to watch his father return to the far end of the boat. He saw him joking with each of the men he passed and felt a new regret that they had never been really close. It wasn't that they got on badly – rather it was a case of living lives that only crossed through domestic routine. Even then, there were weeks when his father was on night duty or something like border duty, when they only saw each other in passing. It had been like this for as long as he could remember. In times of tension or danger, his father relied on him to support and reassure his mother. It was an unspoken commission but both father and son recognised its value and importance. His father never talked about his work and discouraged too many direct questions. In one sense he could easily have been going to work in an office or factory. He never wore uniform going to or from the house and when asked what his father worked at, like all policemen's sons, he automatically replied that he was a civil servant.

But things were not always quite so normal. As the boat nosed through the waves he remembered the morning four years earlier when he had picked up an envelope from the hall floor and felt through it the hard outline of a bullet. They had packed and moved into temporary accommodation within the week. He had come to accept disruption as one of the persistent possibilities of his life.

In the distance now he could see the Copelands. He wondered if anyone still lived on them. There were times in his own life when living on an island would have had its attractions. Almost as if he had been reading his thoughts, one of the men, a sergeant called Alec, turned to him and answered his unspoken question.

'There's nobody living on them now. Nothing there except a few derelict cottages. Hardly worth the effort of making the trip out to them. Know a few boys, though, I'd like to maroon on them.'

They both laughed gently at the joke.

'I believe you're thinking of going to university.'

'If I get the grades, that is – it'll be tough enough.'

'So you're not thinking of following your old man's footsteps and joining the force?'

'No, I don't think so. One policeman in the family is probably all my mother could handle.'

'I know what you mean, son. Anyway, I think your dad would rather see you go on with your education. I want my lad to do the same.'

'You work with my dad, don't you?'

'That's right – know him from a long way back.'

There was a pause while he searched the sea for words.

'Your father's one of the best – they don't come any better, or any straighter. There's not a man on this boat wouldn't follow him anywhere he asked and there's more than one of us wouldn't be here at all if it wasn't for the same man.'

The sincerity behind the testimonial stirred a feeling of pride in him, but also triggered a tremor of doubt about his own frequent indifference. He could think of no reply, but as he looked up, he saw that none was expected, and the conversation slipped into the safe waters of trivia. As he talked about nothing in particular his thoughts tried to focus on his perception of his father. It was difficult for a son to know his father. He sought consolation by thinking of the future and the opportunities that time would bring. Perhaps there could be more trips like this – more outings, more shared times. Maybe they could take up fishing properly and get away for a weekend every so often. The three of them could go together – somewhere quiet and unspoiled, somewhere safe. Maybe even go to the lakes and hire a boat. He would suggest it later on that night. It felt like a good idea, and something told him his father would be pleased by it. Wanting to please his father was a foreign impulse that he hadn't felt since he was a young child. He wondered if it would prove a temporary one.

The roll of the boat jolted his memory and reminded him of the resentment he had felt at various times in the past, caused by his father's non-appearances on a catalogue of occasions – sports days, parents' evenings, cup games. Now he felt that his resentment had been unfair and selfish, realising that the absences bespoke not indifference, but a duality of commitment and responsibility he had never fully appreciated until this moment. He felt a little guilty about the times when he had sought to punish his father by excluding him from information and senti-ments that he shared exclusively with his mother. It had been a childish thing to do. He wondered what his father had felt about it – had it hurt him as intended? There was no way of knowing. He realised too, for the first time, that his father was also part of another family, a family that he knew little about, but whose ties and bonds were equally strong and affectionate.

His thoughts were interrupted by raucous laughter and ironic cheering. One of the men was hanging over the side and being enthusiastically sick, his sea-sickness making him the butt of a rapid succession of schoolboy jokes and vulgar advice, a source of humour that would obviously be milked for weeks to come. He didn't feel all that good himself, but he breathed in deeply and was determined that he would not disgrace himself. Steadying himself with one hand, he lifted his head into the air and felt the cool breeze spray his face.

The sea seemed menacing and restless now. The lights of the boat streaked the encroaching gloom as they reached the mysterious spot, invisibly and inexplicably marked as the destination. The engine cut out and the boat drifted rhythmically with the tide. Immediately, there was a feverish outbreak of activity among the party as they rushed to cast their lines. He let out his own line and watched it spin endlessly into the dark waters.

The room felt artificially empty and silent. Through the window behind the chair he could see one section of the playground. A boy was loitering suspiciously by the bicycle sheds, while pages ripped from a discarded exercise book spiralled aimlessly in the winter wind. In the distance he could see a straggling line of cross-country runners lapping the rugby pitches. The steady, upright posture of the leading pack contrasted with the stooped forms of those following. It looked cold outside. This was the second time he had sat in the headmaster's office. On the first occasion his parents had been with him. By now the experience of moving to a new school had taken on something of a ritual quality. He hoped this one would be the last. Doing A levels was difficult enough without the added burden of being moved in the middle of a course.

His eyes focused on the desk in front of him. The clutter of papers and documents seemed inappropriate, somehow, for what was the holy of holies. What had obviously started as separate piles had merged into one undefined sprawl. A red desk diary lay open and revealed a page of tiny black writing. The cushioned chair behind the desk looked warm and comfortable. He wondered where the headmaster was. Perhaps he was out of school. Outside, in the secretary's office, he could hear voices whispering. He did not need to hear what they were saying to know the reason for his summons. There had been something strange about the vice-principal's mumbled incoherence when he had collected him from the history class, a feeling reinforced by the embarrassed silence during their walk to the head's study. When they had finally reached it, he had been shown in and told that

153

someone would be with him in a few minutes. The few minutes stretched on. The whispering grew louder. The couple of words he was able to catch were enough to confirm what he already knew. He felt now as if a kind of dream was unfolding before his eyes. They were debating whose responsibility it was to tell him. He felt a powerful urge to run out of the room before someone had the chance to pronounce the words he could not bear to hear, the words that would confirm the truth that his heart burned to deny. His memory tortured him with raw images of ripped-apart wreckage of cars, their remains strewn across countless fields. He hoped it had not been like that. His thoughts turned to his mother and he knew he must go to her. Outside the door the whispering had stopped.

The night was growing colder now. The boat's lights shimmered the dark waters. Far off, the lights of the shore signalled their silent invitation. Soon it would be time to return. He was glad, as by now the cool night air was beginning to seep into his bones. The spirits of the men were still high, but his own had begun to sag a little. The monotonous roll of the boat bedded itself uneasily in his balance and his feet began to yearn for firmer ground. The catch itself had been unspectacular and each fish that had been caught was the subject of boisterous celebration. His own lack of success did not concern him and he was content now to be a passive spectator to the proceedings. His father chided him good-humouredly about his lack of luck and proudly held up his own small catch for inspection. He wondered why his father bothered to keep them as he remembered his mother's exasperated refusal to clean and store a previous catch in the family freezer. His smile as his father childishly clutched his trophies spread to a grin when he was offered one 'to pass himself' when he got home.

Overhead, the sky webbed like a black net and stars shivered through its unfathomable depths. The night tensed, taut and motionless. The gulls grew more frantic in their scavenging. A sharp tug on his line awoke him suddenly and he knew at once that he had caught something. His father whooped encouragement, and his arm resting on his shoulder bespoke an equal friendship he had never felt before. Slowly and steadily he reeled in the line. It seemed unending. All eyes were on him and he felt nervous in case he let his father down by doing something clumsily and letting the catch slip away. He wound in, and wondered what was on the end of the line. Then, after a white splash of water, his father slapped his back and the rest of the men cheered as he swung the fish on board. The large fish, silver-wet and smooth, thrashed at his feet, gasping for the sweetness of life. He watched it wordlessly, then turned his head away, as the cold and bitter hook tore remorselessly at the soft chambers of his heart.

THE SILVER SALOON

I THINK it was only my second visit to Belfast. My uncle had asked me to come with him to help make a delivery to some contact of his. When the delivery was made, he dumped me in the city centre and arranged to pick me up in a couple of hours. I think he had a woman to see, but he never gave anything away and I didn't ask.

I had been wandering about aimlessly for an hour when I came across it. It was called The Silver Saloon and the front doors were opened back so that you could walk straight in from the street. Now, when I was younger, we sometimes went on day-trips to Portrush or Ballycastle, and there had been amusement arcades of course, but none had been like this. In those, everything had cost a penny and they had been friendly, haphazard novelties which you were never quite sure were going to work when you put your money in. There was the crane that picked up sweets and always seemed to let the things go just when you were about to win; the bagatelle games where you pulled a lever and propelled a ball round and round until it dropped into a hole with a number on it; and the table-football games where the players were little badly painted dolls covered in woollen rags. There had been fortune-telling machines and machines where they told your future by the strength of your grip, and everything was encased in wooden boxes with glass fronts. Hanging side by side on the wall were cases containing horrific scenes which you paid a penny to activate. My favourite was the execution scene. Curtains were drawn back, a light came on, and a little figure was guillotined, with its head falling into a wooden basket before the curtains closed again. It all took place inside about fifteen seconds, and

157

sometimes you made it do it two or three times, not because you enjoyed seeing someone being decapitated, but because it was really funny when the little head fell off. I used to wonder how they got the head back on. I suppose it was done by magnets. Then there was the graveyard scene where the moon came out, a grave opened, and Dracula appeared wearing his black cloak. I liked that one too.

But The Silver Saloon bore no resemblance to any amusement arcade I had ever been in. For a start, it had a carpet – covered in black cigarette burns, but a carpet nevertheless – and the smell wasn't that fairground mixture of sparks, candy floss and sea, but something completely different, and there was music playing in the background. Everything was new and self-confident, made from shiny coloured metals and plastic, screaming at you to put money in. The lights were white and bright and flashed in the long strips of mirrors and dazzled and blinded. Everything wanted to take your money without giving anything back. Fruit machines with rolling, drunken eyes stuttered along the walls and small women with piled beehive hairdos pulled levers and fed more money without stopping to draw breath or look about them, and when their children tugged at the hems of their imitation leopard-skin coats, they slipped them a few coins without saying anything and the children disappeared for another while.

Down the centre of the hall was a series of large games with clear plastic domes. Spectators and players grouped round them and hung over them. The first one was a model racecourse with five coloured horses. You had to select one and place your money on it before the race began. Then they raced round the track and over little fences and past the winning post. It was just like the real races, only you didn't lose or win so much money, and you won or lost it in exactly twenty seconds. And of course everyone thought they had a system and knew the winning sequence, told their friends which horse to place their money on, and smiled complacently when they were right and looked indignant when they were wrong. Behind it was a basketball game. A rubber ball fell into little numbered sockets and when you pushed the button with the same number it flew towards the basket. I wanted to try this but you needed a partner to play it. There were pinball tables with ringing bells, flashing lights and whirling scoreboards, and all their patrons held on grimly to the sides as if they were exorcising them.

In the bottom half of the room was another racing game, the same type as the first one, only this time it had greyhounds instead of racehorses, and they chased a little plastic hare round the course past a stand full of people, towards their handlers who were standing waiting at the finishing line in white coats. Every twenty seconds there was one winner and four losers, but all the little men in white coats seemed to be smiling. And beside the racing game were the 'Penny Waterfalls' and a huge 'Roll-a-Penny' game. In the 'Roll-a-Penny' you had to roll a penny down a chute on to moving lanes marked in black. If your penny landed in a lane without touching either of the sides, you won the amount marked in that lane, but it was difficult because the lanes were almost the same width as a penny. It was the same principle as the hula-hoop stand – more sophisticated, of course, but really the same. They didn't have a hula-hoop stall, but in that game you have to get the hoop cleanly over the whole prize to win and the prizes are always sitting on thick little blocks, which makes it more difficult than it first appears. But there weren't any hula-hoop stands or any of those types of stalls that needed people to run them.

I had some money in my pocket and I went over to get it changed. It was confusing because usually in arcades there is a woman sitting with hundreds of little carefully counted piles of money in front of her. But this was different. When I told the woman what I wanted, she made no reply, but took my money, leaving me to stand staring expectantly until I received an impatient prod in my back from an elderly woman behind me whose thin finger pointed into a little tray where my pennies waited. I gathered them quickly, dropped one on the floor and had to scramble after it, only recovering it in time to watch her change come cascading out of the machine and scurry down the chute into the little tray.

Turning round to look at the machine, I was momentarily stunned by the lights and the noise, the flashing colours and the bright, white teeth which threatened to bite if you didn't play them. But there was no mystery in the playing, no enjoyment, and the activity was coldly speculative. I played the 'Roll-a-Penny' and lost each time, and of course as soon as the first penny is lost then you're no longer playing for profit but to recoup your losses, and you no longer play with casual indifference, which is the only way that we can come close to catching Chance, who is herself indifferent and spontaneous and has no memory. You see, I understand about luck. Sometimes, for example, when I was kicking a ball about in the garden, I would set a stick in the ground and try to knock it over with the ball. The stick was small and I would stand a good distance away so mostly I would miss. But sometimes after doing this for a while, I would decide to stop, and before walking off would turn and, without looking or thinking, kick the ball, and very often that small stick would fly into the air. To be a winner on luck you have to stop trying. When you try too hard, you always lose. I mean, when you start practising a skill like hitting a stick with a ball or a tin can with a stone, you think about it too much, your brain gets in the way and you start consciously co-ordinating your arms and your legs and balance, with calculations of speed, force and distance. You begin to do things which your whole body can do instinctively for itself and without thinking.

The machines were addictive, filling the head with unfulfilled promises, urging seductively that you have just one more go and whispering that your luck has changed. There was no way that anyone could ever make money out of the machines. If you did win, you only won back what you had already lost, and if you made a winning you ended up losing it again. The only possible way to beat the machines was to walk in, make an immediate win and walk straight out again, but how many people have you ever seen doing that? There was no way that you could beat them – I knew that and yet I still kept feeding my money into them. They could not be beaten because they were machines and had no feelings of greed or loss, and their brains were whirling wheels and tiny cogs.

I lost half my money and was playing 'The Penny Waterfall' when I noticed the man on my left playing the same machine. He was about fifty and was wearing a dark suit. Everything about him was neat and finely cut and there was a slight trace of scent. He seemed intent on what he was doing and from time to time made exasperated little clicking noises, then, without looking at me or taking his eyes off the machine, he said, 'We don't seem to be having much luck, do we?' I agreed with him, surprised that he had even noticed I was there.

'I wouldn't be surprised, you know, if these machines were fixed,' he said.

For a second I thought about explaining how chance worked, but I simply said that he was probably right. Then he turned and smiled at me and his teeth were small and even and white and his eyes were cold and blue. He began talking in his quiet, polite voice and the smell of his scent grew stronger, and in his tie a little diamond tie-pin caught the light and glittered. He said that the waterfall game reminded him of the time he had visited Niagara Falls and what an impressive sight it had been, and how photographs really didn't do it justice. Then he told me about some man who had once walked a tight-rope across it and then returned and carried his manager on his back. This last bit seemed pretty hard to believe, but he didn't look the type of person who would need to tell lies to strangers. Then he put another penny in the machine and won ten back. He seemed pleased in a childish sort of way, and said that I had brought him luck. He asked me if I would like to play the basketball game and said that he would be very grateful if I could give him a game. We played it twice and he paid both times, giving sharp little shrieks of delight or dismay at each score, and all the time he went on talking in his quiet, polite voice about places he had visited and things which he had seen. I said that he seemed to have travelled a good deal, and he said that he had, and that he was something of a 'restless spirit', and when he said this he gave a little laugh which sounded like the tinkling of china. We played a few of the other machines and sometimes he pretended he didn't know how to play and got me to explain it to him, and when he won he insisted that I shared the win because I had brought him luck.

At first he was interesting in a slight sort of way, mainly because I have never travelled and so it was interesting to hear of the places he had visited. But gradually I began to grow tired of him and looked for a way of leaving. His talk began to take on a more serious and moralistic tone and he rebuked young people for their lack of manners and their rudeness to their elders, saying he was certain that parents should discipline them more. He exempted me from this and said how nice it was to meet such a well-mannered young man, and as he relaxed again he asked me to have a go on the shooting range. They didn't have one of those ranges where you fire at little rows of moving ducks, but there was a submarine game in the shape of a periscope where you looked into a darkened screen and fired at moving battleships. I missed my first few shots and, saying that he would help me, he stood close behind me, and, looking over my shoulder, placed his hand on top of mine. His hand was small and fine, and I felt his breath on my neck and smelt the sickly swirl of his scent. I was glad when the game finished and I said that I had to go. Without waiting for a reply I turned and walked towards the door. Trying to appear casual, I strolled slowly down the hall, stopping occasionally to look briefly at some machine. I did not look back.

When I got outside I began to walk quickly but I had only gone a short distance when someone grabbed me and bundled me into a doorway. There were four of them. They were younger and smaller than me and had the smell of poverty about them. They had been in The Silver Saloon and must have followed me when I left. The leader grabbed my shirt collar with a black hand and held a fist close to my nose.

'Giv' us yer money,' he demanded, half-closing one eye as he said it.

'I haven't got any,' I stammered, staring at his feet.

Then the other started mimicking my country accent and calling me a country yokel.

'Giv'us yer money or I'll do ya!' threatened the leader as he pulled my shirt tighter.

I took the few coins left in my pocket and handed them over, almost apologising for not having more. One of the others grabbed my lapel and asked me if I was a Prod. I sensed from the question that they were not, and so I said I was a Catholic.

'Say your rosary!' they demanded.

When they found out my lie, the four pummelled me to the ground, each taking a kick before they ran off. I picked myself up and dusted my clothes, feeling only the hot surge of anger and shame.

THE PLEASURE DOME

THE CAR'S wipers pushed the rain aside, smearing the windscreen with a transfer of glazed light and colour. Rhythmically and hypnotically, like the beat of a drum, they moved from side to side, clearing the constant splashes before their replacements could stipple the glass. Colours, strange colours – purples, blues, reds – bled into the fluorescent yellow of street lamps and distorted the streets into a vibrant, translucent wash. Few people emerged from the shadows – a group of youths huddled at a street corner, a couple hurrying somewhere, an old man carrying a bicycle wheel. Momentary glimpses, then swept away in a fan of spray. Yellow light ran into white and back into yellow, streaking the road with slivers of neon that glittered like lights on a Christmas tree. Still the rain slanted down and still the wipers pushed it aside, silently and indifferently, like the blink of a giant eye that looked out from the car's darkness and drank the transient images that flashed before it. Streams of silver water swirled in the gutter. The eye blinked. A woman with a black umbrella silently gestured her lagging child to stay beneath its shelter. The child trailed behind, splashing in a puddle, the coloured droplets frozen eternally in a dream. A confusion of streets and roads engulfed them, the strange and familiar merging and blending into one rivulet of refraction, transforming city, car and music into one prismatic pulse.

The car moved erratically on its course with unpredictable speed and control. The driver had still not mastered the gears and his uncertainty produced a series of jerks and screeches. The car had looked new and attractive, but its multiplicity of switches and lights made the dashboard swim before his muddled senses and for an instant caused him to regret their choice. Perhaps they should have been less ambitious but the open invitation had proved impossible to reject. He knew its conspicuous appearance was dangerous, but could not resist its streamlined beauty. Black cars always reminded him of American films and streets in cities like New York or San Francisco. It had been the colour that had finally persuaded his already willing spirit. He imagined himself the hero of a film, invisible cameras recording his every action and expression.

The music was a bonus. It pounded out of the expensive invisible speakers, a soundtrack to the film, and throbbed with an incessant and inescapable beat. There was, too, a variety of tapes to choose from, shop-bought tapes with real music by current groups and not the usual trash of James Last or country and western. The car belonged to someone young. He felt a bitter resentment that such a car could be owned by someone who still had young blood running in his veins. As he took a slug of wine – its sourness no longer noticeable to his tongue – his left hand beat the steering wheel's rim in rhythm to the music. His passenger looked at him, his face bright and elated.

'This is friggin' magic, Joe, real class. Will you let me drive soon?'

His pleasure spilled out in whoops of crazed exuberance. Joe supposed he would have to let him drive soon – it was only fair – but not just yet.

'Soon, okay? I'm just beginning to get the feel of her. She's different from anything we've had before. Faster, smoother – a real flier. Put another tape on.'

Roon rummaged in the cassette case, his mouth and eyes widening in concentration as he read out the names and titles. He had no confidence that his own selection would please the driver.

'Frankie Goes to Hollywood,' ordered Joe, sensing his companion's confusion.

'Hey, Joe, we could go to Hollywood if we wanted to – "Joe and Roon Go to Hollywood" – screw Frankie, nobody invited him.'

He laughed at his own joke and the rain fell heavily, sealing the car off from the world outside. The words and music of 'Welcome to the Pleasure Dome' rumbled through the speakers like manic thunder. Involuntarily, their hands and feet pounded out the swelling beat. The eye blinked once again. A black taxi squealed to a stop and, like some conjurer's illusion, an impossible number of people piled out from its inside; some boys in identical grey jerkins stood break-dancing in a shop doorway. Roon squinted round and stared like a deaf man. Then they were gone, washed away in a wave of liquid neon. The car moved on. Miles of roads. Long corridors of shops, the derelict and the new nestling side by side. Ten thousand streets, identical veins off identical arteries, deserted, sheltering from the storm, television light spearing the gloom.

The car came to a halt at a temporary red light. Roadworks ahead were heralded by neat lines of cones. A single file of traffic came towards them. The light stayed red. No cars. Impatience rustled and grew until a foot pressed the accelerator and they sped forward on the red. Roon pushed his feet hard to the floor, pressing imaginary brakes and slipped down in the seat until only the top of his head was visible from behind. A white van started down the single traffic lane and then, brakes screeching, skidded to a quivering halt as the black car sliced violently across its front. Cones showered in the air. Horns blared. More cones rolled drunkenly askew. The wipers seemed almost drowned by spray and rain. For a few seconds the car twisted out of control and then gouged the side of a parked car like a tin-opener before righting itself and speeding on.

'Shit, Joe! You're a bloody madman!'

Roon was shaken but no longer frightened. From the driver's seat came a gentle laugh. The music reimposed itself. As they turned into a side street, Joe recited in a serious voice, as if fearful of getting the words wrong: 'In Xanadu did Kubla Khan a stately pleasure-dome decree, where Alph, the sacred river, ran through caverns measureless to man down to a sunless sea.'

'What you talking about, Joe? Those aren't the words.'

167

'That's where the song comes from – the poem 'Kubla Khan'. You don't think that lot thought it up for themselves, do you?'

'A poem, Joe? I thought it was just a song.'

'It's a poem – didn't you do it in school?'

'We never did poetry – we didn't do anything in school. Non-exam class from first form. Projects – that was all we ever did. Things like 'The History of Manchester United' or 'The World of Animals'. You know – tracing pictures from books, copying out chunks till your arm was sore, sticking in photocopies with those poxy little Pritt sticks (they never trusted you with glue). After a while it really pissed me off and you always knew they never really marked them. No matter what it was like, you got a "B" and a "Good effort made". The bastards never read them, Joe.'

Roon slumped back into the seat momentarily exhausted by his eloquence and wounded by the memory. Joe drove on in silence.

'We never got poetry, Joe – just projects and community service.'

Joe laughed.

'What community service have you ever done, Roon?'

'Decorating old people's homes and things like that.'

'Casing them, more like.'

'I never stole nothing. Honest I didn't. I liked doing it. Some of those old people were all right – made you tea and talked to you about things. I never stole nothing.'

His feelings hurt, Roon slipped into a protective womb of silence and hunched his knees up on the seat. The car drove on, unravelling the twisted knot of streets, glazing the somnolent pavements with a lustre of spray.

'You never missed anything, Roon. Poetry was shit. You remember hardman McGuinness – he made me learn the thing for talking in his class. The bastard didn't let up until I could recite the whole thing word perfect. It went on for about a month. Once I'd learnt it I couldn't forget it.'

Roon was appeased.

'Honest, Joe, I never stole anything.'

'If McGuinness was to walk out now in front of this car I'd run him over like a dog.'

'He was a dog all right – a bloody mad dog. You remember the day he butted Rory Mallon? Split him open like a pod of peas. They say when his da came up McGuinness grabbed him by the throat and nearly throttled him. Almost went to court until Gallagher bought him off.'

'If he walked out now off that pavement no money in the world'd buy me off. I'd have him.'

He pressed his foot hard to the floor, making it thrust forward with a throaty curse of angry revs. The rain had eased a little now. In the blink of the eye appeared an old woman with an umbrella, a man with a muzzled greyhound, a sodden flag lashed to a lamp post; on waste ground two dogs sniffing round a black polythene bag. Then they crossed a bridge taking them into unfamiliar areas. Roon felt it was his turn to drive now but hesitated to ask again.

'What's a pleasure dome anyway, Joe?'

Joe thought before he answered.

'It's a kind of special city this ruler ordered to be built with special things in it. It's difficult to describe it and anyway, it wasn't real – it was just made up.'

'Was it a bit like Disneyland?'

'Yeah, a bit like that,' laughed Joe.

'Ross McShane's been to Disneyland. When we were in primary school, ten kids got selected to go on this trip to America. The family he was staying with took him. He said it was class. He said you could spend a week there and not see everything that was in it.'

'How come you didn't get picked, Roon?'

'Aw, you know the form. They only took the goodies. They were supposed to take the most deserving but they sent all the teachers' pets. It was supposed to be for kids who never had a holiday and they sent Ross McShane – everybody knows his da's got a bloody caravan in Millisle.'

'Have you ever had a holiday, Roon?' asked Joe.

'Once I went with our Jim to see a match in Liverpool and a couple of years ago I had a weekend in Buncrana with the youth club. I wouldn't've minded going to America though. It wasn't bloody fair, Joe – everyone knows his da's got a caravan.'

'Forget it. Anyway, you're on your holiday now. Enjoy yourself.'

He passed his companion the almost empty bottle and watched him drain it dry.

'Joe, McShane said Disneyland's bigger than Belfast. Do you think he was lying?'

'Course he was – the lying wee git. If you see the wee shit let me know and we'll flatten him like a pancake. He probably never even seen Disneyland.'

'You're too right. The closest McShane ever got to Disneyland was watching cartoons on friggin' TV. Next time I see him I'm going to tell him that to his face.'

The car drove on, exploring unfamiliar territory, their tribal instincts both disturbed and excited by the foreignness of their surroundings. Soon it would be time to return. Soon it would be time to ditch the car. But not just yet. The rain had eased now and filtered into a fine drizzle, allowing the wipers to relax a little and the eye to focus with greater clarity. A small flock of the faithful congregated round an open-air meeting, the preacher's Bible raised above his head; the green neon telephone number of a taxi firm branded the dusk; two youngsters kicked a ball against a gable wall. A man came out of a Chinese takeaway with a brown paper bag. The car circled a roundabout several times, unsure of which direction to take, then headed off on a route that seemed to point them towards familiar hunting grounds.

On a street corner ahead stood a gang of youths, restless and bored by the rain's confinement. Two kicked a tin can to each other in a parody of seriousness. A different tribe. Roon lowered his window and pointed wordlessly at the empty bottle. The car closed to the kerb and reduced its speed. Twisting his body as far as the restriction of the seat would allow, he flung the bottle at the group. It fell short but sprayed glass in their direction, the noise and uncertainty of the nature of the missile sending them scuttling into the depths of doorways for safety.

'A present from Walt Disney!' shouted Roon as the car sped off, their laughter echoing each other's.

The moment gave impetus to their recklessness. The shelter of the car created a feeling of security and the steady rhythm of the music soothed all fears of apprehension. They accelerated past cars on the inside, then weaved in and out of others, a scream of horns and brakes cursing in their wake.

'Look out, mister – it's the Dukes of Hazzard!' shouted Roon, whooping and cheering like a cowboy at a rodeo and waving ironically to each new victim. He wanted to drive more than anything, but was frightened to ask. Joe was the boss, strange and unpredictable, but definitely the boss. He would not disturb him now, when he was in a mood that seemed close to happiness. Happiness was a mood that was a rare visitor to his friend, and he would not risk chasing it away. He whooped again as the car boomed through a large pool of water, hurling spray skywards like a bursting firework.

The rain came on heavily again. The windscreen smeared and glazed again, colours sliding into one another in a stained blue of swimming neon. The eye struggled to blink. A wall shouted white-painted words and dates. Roon, searching the dashboard, found a pair of sunglasses and stared out at the greyness. An almost empty bus stopped on the opposite side of the road and an old man got off. No one got on.

'It'd be good, Joe, if we never had to go back. It'd be good if we could keep this one and just keep going. This is the best one we've ever had – why don't we keep it, Joe?'

'Don't be stupid, Roon. How long do you think we'd last before they found us? There's not many cars like this driving around. We should've ditched it long ago.'

'I don't want to go back, Joe. There's plenty of petrol in the tank – why don't we take her and go somewhere really far? Drive all night. We could share the driving and whenever you get tired I could take over – just until you were ready again.'

'Where'd we go? Sure you don't know your way round

anywhere outside your own street. You're like a fish out of water once you leave your own patch – you'd be girning to go home five minutes after you'd got there.'

Behind the sunglasses Roon's eyes widened in denial.

'No I wouldn't. No way, Joe. What've I got to go back for? I don't have nothing back there and neither do you. Why don't we do it? We could go to Millisle and stay in Ross McShane's caravan and in the morning we could hitch it on the back of the car and take it with us. We could do it, Joe. What do you say?'

'You're crazy, Roon, wired-to-the-moon crazy. How'd we know which caravan was McShane's? Have you never seen those caravan parks? – there's hundreds of bloody caravans and they all look the same. We're going back now before it's too late. With your record, you'll go inside if you're caught – have you thought of that?'

Roon slumped into defeated silence. The tape ended but he made no attempt to replace it, staring forlornly out of the passenger window like a prisoner on his way to the condemned cell. A rectangle of yellow light fractured the greyness as the entrance to a social club was held open by a doorman. Three middle-aged women emerged, struggling with coats and hand-bags. A young boy came out of a side street carrying a snooker cue, then two girls dressed in yellow and orange with ribbons in their hair. A bicycle tyre necklaced a street lamp.

'Going inside doesn't worry me,' he replied in a slow and sullen voice. 'It isn't so bad. Colin O'Neill said it was a dead-on place and he's been there often enough to know. So it doesn't worry me.'

'Anything would seem better to Colin O'Neill than where he lives. Have you ever seen it? It's a real pit. He probably thinks he's been sent to a holiday camp. He's a real big-time gangster and all. Burning down mobile classrooms or doing old age pensioners' meters – that's about O'Neill's limit. He probably only does it to get sent away.'

Despite all his efforts, Roon could not stop himself grinning. The grin dispelled his despondency and he reverted to his original mood. As a couple of girls stood waiting to cross the road, he rolled the window down and shouted an intimate greeting that caused them to turn their heads away and giggle with enjoyed embarrassment.

'Hey, Joe, we could touch for real class with a car like this. No scrubbers – just real class. They'd be fighting each other to get off with us. We could have our pick.'

'Girls is only trouble – you're better off without them. Take my advice – stay away from them, Roon. They spend your money and when it's gone they're after someone else.'

'They'll not spend my money – I never have any. It must feel good, though, to have a good-looking girl on your arm. The guy who owns this probably has a different one every night. Real class looks and clothes, the lot. Probably does the business right there in the back seat. What you think, Joe?'

There was no answer. Joe sat still and silent, his eyes flicking repeatedly to the mirror and his hands tightening on the wheel. He wasn't sure. It was too early to do anything that would distinguish them from other cars and yet he needed to be ready. He let Roon go on talking – there was no point in panicking him. He might be mistaken. It was important not to panic. Even if it was a police car it didn't mean that they were being followed, and it might just as well be a routine patrol, totally unaware of their existence. Reducing their speed, he drove carefully and correctly, meekly staying in the inside lane, and as they approached the first turn-off he signalled and left the main road. His first glance in the mirror told him it was a police car and they were being followed. Automatically, his foot pressed down on the accelerator and the car surged forward. Roon's unspoken question was answered by a sideways flick of the head and still more speed. As understanding filtered through to him, he slid lower into the seat and braced his feet against the front of the car. Joe expected, and partly wished, it to be like the films, but no sirens screeched hysterically or lights flashed, only a reciprocal increase of speed and steady pursuit.

The street flashed by in a blur of rain-washed speed, and then another and another, each a perfect echo, unwinding and ravelling in a matted nightmare. Sweet Jesus – a dark figure stepped out from between parked cars . . . an instinctive swerve and the narrowest of misses. Every corner, brakes and gears screaming their angry protest. Directionless, following the road, taking corners blind, fear in the throat and churning the stomach. Holy orisons to an unloved God, swear words bursting out like the dispersal of bitter seed; a million Hail Marys – a promise of countless candles burning brightly in the intensity of momentary sincerity. An old man on a bicycle, unsteady, wobbling in confusion before falling on to the pavement and hitting his head. Children standing open-mouthed and staring before indifference washed over them and sent them back to the reality of play.

Roon looked at his companion and was frightened by his expressionless stare. Then he whimpered and squirmed more tightly into the seat.

'I'm scared, Joe. I don't want to go inside. Colin O'Neill said the first thing that happens is they give you a kicking, then they lock you away on your own for days. I'd go crazy, Joe.'

He started to cry.

'No one's going to give you a kicking. Trust me, Roon. They can't take us while we stay in these streets. If we can lose them for a few minutes we're not far from home, then we can bale out and run for it. Now, stop crying and get that cloth and keep the windows from steaming up.'

The car's headlights sparked a dog's eyes into fire. Roon, happier with a task to concentrate on, rubbed furiously at the windows as if intent on polishing the glass. Suddenly and inexplicably, they found themselves in a dead-end – a one-sided street of blocked-up derelict houses. Opposite stretched a vast open area levelled for redevelopment where already some work had started and a building site had been established. Without hesitation, he vaulted the car into the heart of the blackness and headed for the distant lights that promised freedom. The car bumped and skidded over pot-holed waste ground strewn with bricks and debris, the two occupants bouncing up and down like riders on a bucking bronco. Roon's legs locked rigid, his eyes closed, and his hands gripped the sides of the seats until his knuckles blanched. His mouth struggled silently to form the words of forgotten prayers. Something large smacked up against the underside of the car, causing it to veer violently to the left before the driver wrestled it back on to its original course. Joe aimed blindly at the lights ahead and fought desperately to keep control of the steering that seemed now to have a wild life of its own. With back wheels skidding, they slithered like a snake over the final stretch, before righting on the road opposite. Then, with a change of gears, they raced in the direction of safety. Unwilling to trust the mirror alone, they both turned sideways in their seats and squinted intently over their shoulders. The road behind them was clear. Roon let rip a shout of unbridled joy and clenched his fists in front of his face like someone who had just scored a match-winning goal. They had made it, and as the realisation broke over them, the tension burst and they drowned in an ecstasy of relief and exhilaration.

'We did it, Joe! We did it! You were bloody magic. Wait till the lads hear about this. Eat your heart out, O'Neill! I thought we'd had it – I really did. It was like something out of a film. You were magic, Joe!'

Joe relaxed in the praise and pumped the car's horn several times to sound a raucous fanfare of celebration, familiar streets and places increasing their feeling of security. The writing on the walls glistened in the wet like letters of love. A feeling almost like regret stirred in his heart. Soon it would be time to ditch the car, and he had grown attached to it. They had been through a good deal together and he couldn't help feeling something akin to loyalty. His hands caressed the wheel and he avoided thinking of its eventual end.

'Well, Roon, you're almost home.'

The eye blinked for the last time. The heart's home; broken glass cemented along the top of a wall like coloured icing on a cake; a wave of wire, twisted and barbed; deserted entries like barren black branches on a winter tree. The heart's home, a crumbling sarcophagus about to crack open.

'Almost there, Roon. Back to our Pleasure Dome. Back to where we belong.' Splashed and dented, the black car crested the empty road. Up ahead the two landrovers partially blocked the street, their blue lights spinning. A police sergeant standing in the middle of the road shuffled his feet nervously and wished the wait was over. A radio crackled with static. The blue lights whirled. In a shop doorway, a policeman shouldered a rifle and turned up his collar against the rain.

ORANGES FROM SPAIN

IT'S NOT a fruit shop any more. Afterwards, his wife sold it and someone opened up a fast food business. You wouldn't recognise it now – it's all flashing neon, girls in identical uniforms and the type of food that has no taste. Even Gerry Breen wouldn't recognise it now. Either consciously or unconsciously, I don't seem to pass that way very often, but when I do I always stop and look at it. The neon brightness burns the senses and sears the memories like a wound being cauterised; but then it all comes back and out flows a flood of memory that nothing can stem.

I was sixteen years old and very young when I went to work for Mr Breen in his fruit shop. It was that summer when it seemed to rain every day and a good day stood out like something special. I got the job through patronage. My father and Gerry Breen went back a long way – that always struck me as strange, because they were so unlike as men. Apparently, they were both born in the same street and grew up together, and even when my father's career as a solicitor took him up-market, they still got together occasionally. My father collected an order of fruit every Friday night on his way home from work, and as children we always talked about 'Gerry Breen's apples'. It's funny the things you remember, and I can recall very clearly my mother and father having an argument about it one day. She wanted to start getting fruit from the supermarket for some reason, but my father wouldn't hear of it. He got quite agitated about it and almost ended up shouting, which was very unlike him. Maybe he acted out of loyalty, or maybe he owed him some kind of favour, but whatever the reason, the arrangement continued.

If his name is mentioned now they never do it in front of me.

It's almost as if he never existed. At first it angered me – it was almost as if they thought I would disintegrate at its sound – but gradually I came to be grateful for it. I didn't even go to the funeral, and from that moment it was obvious my family sought to draw a curtain over the whole event. My mother had taken me away for a week's holiday. We stayed with one of her sisters who lives in Donegal, and I've never had a more miserable time. Inevitably, it rained every day and there was nothing to do but mope around and remember, trapped in a house full of women, where the only sounds were the clink of china cups and the click of knitting needles. It was then the dreams started. The intervening years have lessened their frequency but not their horror. When I woke up screaming for about the tenth time, they took me to a special doctor who reassured them with all the usual platitudes – I'd grow out of it, time was a great healer, and so on. In one sense I did grow out of it – I stopped telling anyone about the nightmares and kept them strictly private. They don't come very often now, but when they do only my wife knows. Sometimes she cradles me in her arms like a child until I fall asleep again.

I hadn't even really wanted a job in the first place. It was all my father's idea. He remembered the long weeks of boredom I had complained about the summer before and probably the nuisance I had been as I lazed about the house. I walked right into his trap. He knew I'd been working up to ask if I could have a motorbike for my next birthday. The signs weren't good, and my mother's instinctive caution would have been as difficult a barrier to surmount as the expense, so it came as a surprise when my father casually enquired if I'd be interested in starting to save for one. I took the bait, and before I knew what was happening, I'd been fixed up with a summer job, working in Gerry Breen's fruit shop.

I didn't like the man much at first. He was rough and ready and he would've walked ten miles on his knees to save a penny. I don't think he liked me much either. The first day he saw me he looked me up and down with unconcealed disappointment, with the expression of someone who'd just bought a horse that wasn't strong enough to do the work he had envisaged for it. He stopped short of feeling my arm muscles, but passed some comment about me needing to fill out a bit. Although he wasn't tall himself, he was squat and had a kind of stocky strength that carried him through every physical situation. You knew that when he put his shoulder to the wheel, the chances were the wheel would spin. He wore this green coat as if it was some sort of uniform, and I never saw him in the shop without it. It was shiny at the elbows and collar, but it always looked clean. He had sandy-coloured hair that was slicked back and oiled down in a style that suggested he had once had an affinity with the Teddy boys. The first time I met him I noticed his hands, which were flat and square, and his chisel-shaped fingers. He had this little red pen-knife, and at regular intervals he used it to clean them. The other habit he had was a continual hitching-up of his trousers, even though there was no apparent prospect of them falling down. He was a man who seemed to be in perpetual motion. Even when he was standing talking to someone, there was always some part of him that was moving, whether it was transferring his pencil from one ear to the other, or hoisting up the trousers. It was as if there was a kind of mechanism inside him. Sometimes I saw him shuffle his feet through three hundred and sixty degrees like some kind of clockwork toy. For him sitting still would have been like wearing a strait-jacket, and I don't think any chair, no matter how comfortable, ever held him for more than a few minutes.

On my first morning, after his initial disappointment had worn off and he had obviously resolved to make the best of a bad job, he handed me a green coat, similar to his own but even older. It had a musty smell about it that suggested it had been hanging in a dark cupboard for some considerable time, and although I took it home that first weekend for my mother to wash, I don't think the smell ever left it. The sleeves were too long, so all summer I wore it with the cuffs turned up. My first job was chopping sticks. As well as fruit and vegetables, he sold various other things, including bundles of firewood. Out in the back yard was a mountain of wood, mostly old fruit boxes, and for the rest of that morning I chopped them into sticks and put them in polythene bags. At regular intervals he came out to supervise the work and caution me with monotonous regularity to be careful with the hatchet. It was obvious I wasn't doing it to his satisfaction; his dissatisfaction was communicated by a narrowing of his eyes and a snakelike hiss. As far as I was concerned, there weren't too many ways you could chop sticks, but I was wrong. Unable to restrain his frustration any longer, he took the hatchet and proceeded to instruct me in the correct technique. This involved gently inserting it into the end of the piece of wood and then tapping the other end lightly on the ground so that it split gently along the grain. When he was assured I had mastered the method, he watched critically over my first efforts.

'Too thick, son, too thick. Did your da never teach you how to chop sticks?'

It was only when I had produced a series of the thinnest slivers that he seemed content. I suppose it meant he got more bundles of firewood, but you wouldn't have got much of a fire out of them. It made me feel guilty somehow, like I was an accessory to his stinginess. 'Did your da never teach you how to?' was a phrase I heard repeatedly that summer, and it inevitably prefaced a period of instruction in the correct technique and subsequent supervision.

The rest of my time that first morning was divided between sweeping up and humping bags of spuds from the yard into the store-room. No matter how often I brushed that shop floor, it always seemed to need to be done again. I must have filled a whole dump with cauliflower leaves, and I never stopped hating that smell. Perhaps, if I'm honest, I felt the job was a little beneath me. By the time the day was over, my back was aching and I was still trying to extract splinters from my hands. The prospect of a summer spent working like that filled me with despondency, and the attraction of a motorbike lost some of its appeal. I thought of telling my father I didn't want to go back, but was stopped by the knowledge that I would have to listen to eternal speeches about how soft young people were, and how they wanted everything on a plate. That I didn't need, and so I resolved to grit my teeth and stick it out.

The shop was situated at the bottom of the Antrim Road, and while it wasn't that big, every bit of space was used, either for display or storage. It started outside on the pavement where each morning, after carrying out wooden trestles and resting planks on them, we set out trays of fruit, carefully arranged and hand-picked, designed to attract and entice the passer-by. Above all this stretched a green canvas canopy which was supported by ancient iron stanchions, black with age. When it rained it would drip on to the front displays of fruit and so all that summer I had to carry them in and out of the shop. Inside was a long counter with old-fashioned scales and a till that rang as loudly as church bells. Under the counter were paper bags of every size, miles of string, metal hooks, bamboo canes, withered yellow rubber gloves, weights, elastic bands and a paraphernalia of utensils of unfathomable purpose. On the wall behind the counter was an assortment of glass-fronted shelving, sagging under the weight of fruit and vegetables. Above head height, the walls were covered in advertising posters that had obviously arrived free with consignments of fruit and looked like they had been there since the shop opened. On the customer side was more shelving and below it a clutter of wooden and cardboard boxes that seemed designed to ladder tights or catch the wheels of shopping trolleys. If there was any kind of logical system in the layout, I never managed to work it out. I got the impression it had evolved into a sprawling disorder and that so long as everything was close at hand, the owner saw no reason to change it.

In the back of the shop was a store-room where among merchandise and debris stood a wooden table, two chairs, a gas cooker and a sink. The only other room was a small washroom. Beyond this was a small cobbled yard, enclosed by a brick wall topped with broken glass. Over everything hung the sweet, ripe smell of a fruit shop, but in Mr Breen's shop it was mixed with a mildewed mustiness, a strange hybrid that stayed in my senses long after I had left the scene.

I worked my butt off that first day and it was obvious he intended getting value for money out of me. Maybe my father had told him it was what I needed – I don't know. It was nearly time to close and the shop was empty. He was working out some calculations on the back of a brown paper bag and I was moving fruit into the store room, when he glanced up at me with a kind of puzzled look, as if he was trying to work out what I was thinking.

'Sure, son, it's money for old rope. Isn't that right?'

I gave a non-committal nod of my head and kept on working. Then he told me I could go, and I could tell he was wondering whether he would see me the next day. Returning to his calculations again, he licked the stub of the pencil he was using and hitched up his trousers. I said goodbye and just as I was going out the door he called me back.

'Do you want to know something, son?'

I looked at him, unsure of what response he expected. Then, signalling me closer, he whispered loudly, 'My best friends are bananas.' I forced a smile at his joke, then walked out into the street and took a deep breath of fresh air.

The fruit shop did steady business. Most of the trade came from the housewives who lived in the neighbourhood, but there was also a regular source of custom from people who arrived outside the shop in cars, and by their appearance didn't live locally – the type who bought garlic. He knew them all by name and sometimes even had their order already made up, always making a fuss over them and getting me to carry it out to their car. They were obviously long-standing customers, and I suppose they must have stayed loyal to him because they were assured of good quality fruit. He had a way with him – I had to admit that. He called every woman 'madam' for a start, even those who obviously weren't, but when he said it, it didn't sound like flattery, or like he was patronising them. It just sounded polite in an old-fashioned way. He had a great line in chat as well. If he didn't know them it was usually some remark about the weather, but if he did, he would ask about their families or make jokes, always cutting his cloth according to his audience. When a gaggle of local women were in, it was all 'Now, come on, ladies, get your grapes. Sweetest you can taste. Just the thing for putting passion into your marriage', or 'Best bananas – good enough to eat sideways'. They all loved it, and I'm sure it was good for business.

Whatever their bills came to, he always gave them back the few odd pence, and I'm sure they thought he was very generous. As far as I was concerned, I thought he was one of the meanest men I'd ever met. For a start, he never threw anything away – that was one of the things that was wrong with the shop. Whether it was a bit of string or a piece of wood, he stored it carefully, and if he saw me about to throw something away, he'd stop me with a 'Never know when it might come in useful, son'. Most of the produce he collected himself from the market early in the morning, but whenever deliveries were made, he inspected each consignment rigorously, with an energy that frequently exasperated the deliverer. If he found a damaged piece of fruit, he would hold it up for mutual observation and, wrestling up his trousers with the other hand, would say something like, 'Now come on George, are you trying to put me out of business?' and he'd haggle anew over already arranged prices. Watching him sniffing out flawed produce would have made you think he'd an in-built radar system. And he was always looking for something for nothing. Sometimes it was embarrassing. If the Antrim Road had still had horses going up and down it, he'd have been out collecting the droppings and selling them for manure.

One day Father Hennessy came into the shop. Mr Breen's face dropped noticeably and about half a dozen parts of his body seemed to fidget all at once.

'Hello, Father. What can I do for you?'

'Hello, Gerry. How's business?'

'Slow, Father, very slow.'

The priest smiled and, lifting an apple, rubbed it on his sleeve, the red bright against the black.

'I'm popping over to the Mater to visit some parishioners. I thought a nice parcel of fruit would cheer them up. Help them to get better.'

He started to eat the apple and his eyes were smiling.

'Of course, Father. A very good idea.'

With well-disguised misery, he parcelled up a variety of fruit and handed it over the counter.

'God bless you, Gerry. Treasure in heaven, treasure in heaven.'

With the package tucked under his arm, and still eating the apple, the priest sauntered out to his car. If he had looked back, he would have seen Mr Breen slumped on the counter, his head resting on both hands.

'The church'll be the ruin of me. He does that about three times a month. Thinks my name's Mr Del Monte, not Gerry Breen. Treasure in heaven's no use to me when I go to pay the bills at the end of the month.'

The frustration poured out of him and I listened in silence, knowing he wasn't really talking to me.

'Does he go up to Michael Devlin in the bank and ask him for some money because he's going to visit the poor? Since when did it become part of my purpose in life to subsidise the National Health system? I pay my taxes like anyone else.'

I think he'd have gone on indefinitely in a similar vein, but for the arrival of a customer, and then it was all smiles and jokes about the rain.

'Do you know, Mrs Caskey, what I and my assistant are building out in the yard?'

Mrs Caskey didn't know but her aroused curiosity was impatient for an answer.

'We're building an ark! And whenever it's finished we're going to load up two of every type of fruit and float away up the road.'

'Get away with you, Gerry. You're a desperate man.'

And then he sold her tomatoes and a lettuce which he described as 'the best lettuce in the shop'. I'd almost have believed him myself, but for the fact that I'd already heard the same phrase on about three previous occasions that day.

Gerry Breen was very proud of his shop, but he took a special pride in his displays outside, and he did this expert printing with whitening on the front window. Not only did he fancy himself a bit of an artist, but also as a kind of poet laureate among fruiterers. He had all these bits of cardboard – I think they were backing cards out of shirts – and on them he printed, not only the names and prices of the fruit, but also descriptive phrases meant to stimulate the taste buds of the reader. Grapes might be described as 'deliciously sweet' or strawberries as 'the sweet taste

of summer' while Comber spuds were always 'balls of flour'.
The front window always looked well. Bedded on a gentle slope
of simulated grass rested the various sections of produce, complete with printed labels. Each morning when he had arranged it
he would go out on the pavement and stand with his hands on
his hips, studying it like an art critic viewing a painting. Inside
he had other signs saying things like 'Reach for a peach',
'Iceberg lettuce – just a tip of the selection' or 'Fancy an apple –
why not eat a pear?'

After the first week or so we started to get on a little better. I
think he realised that I was trustworthy and prepared to pull my
weight. He probably thought of me as being a bit snobbish, but
tolerated it so long as he got good value for his money. I in turn
became less critical of what I considered his defects. Gradually,
he began to employ more of my time on less menial jobs. After
three weeks I had progressed to serving customers and weighing
their fruit, and then a week later I was allowed to enter the holy
of holies and put my hand in the till. I still had to chop sticks
and brush up of course, but whenever the shop was busy I
served behind the counter. I almost began to feel part of the
business. The continual wet weather stopped me from missing
out on the usual activities of summer and I was increasingly
optimistic that my father would reward my industry with a
motorbike. Mr Breen didn't much like the rain – he was always
complaining how bad it was for business. According to him, it
discouraged passing trade, and people didn't buy as much as
they did in warm weather. He was probably right. Sometimes,
when a lull in trade created boredom, I tried to wind him up a
little.

'Mr Breen, do you not think it's wrong to sell South African
fruit?'

'Aw, don't be daft, son.'

'But do you not think that by selling their fruit you're supporting apartheid?'

He swopped his pencil from ear to ear and did what looked a
bit like a tap dance.

'I'm only supporting myself and the wife. Sure wouldn't the

blacks be the first to suffer if I stopped selling it? They'd all end up starving and how would that help them?'

I was about to provoke him further when a customer appeared and I let him have the last word.

'God knows, son, they have my sympathy – don't I work like a black myself?'

The customer turned out to be Mr Breen's wife. She was all dressed up in a blue and white suit and was on her way to some social function. She had one of those golden charm bracelets that clunked so many heavy charms I wondered how her wrist bore the strain, and while she hardly looked sideways at him, she made an embarrassing fuss over me, asking about my parents and school, and gushing on in a slightly artificial way. When she finished whatever business she had, she said goodbye to me and warned Gerald not to work me too hard. I smiled at the name Gerald, and I could see him squirming behind the counter. A heavy shower came on and we both stood in the doorway watching it bounce off the road. He was unusually silent and I glanced at him a few times to see if he was all right. When he spoke, his voice was strangely colourless.

'Never get married, son – it's the end of your happiness.'

I didn't know whether he was joking or not, so I just went on staring at the rain.

'My wife's ashamed of me,' he said in the same lifeless voice.

I uttered some vague and unconvincing disagreement and then turned away in embarrassment. I started to brush the floor, glancing up from time to time as he stood motionless in the doorway. In a minute or so the rain eased and it seemed to break the spell, but for the rest of that afternoon, he was subdued and functioned in a mechanical way. He even closed the shop half an hour early – something he'd never done before.

Nothing like that ever happened again, and my first experience of work slipped into an uneventful routine. One day, though, comes clearly to mind. One afternoon when business was slack he asked me to deliver fruit round to a Mrs McCausland. The address was a couple of streets away and I felt a little self-conscious as I set off in my green coat. It wasn't a big order – just a few apples and oranges and things. I followed the directions I had been given and arrived at a terraced house. Unlike most of its neighbours, the front door was closed, and the net curtain in the window offered no glimpse of the interior. At first, it seemed as if no one was in, and I was just about to turn and leave, when there was the slow undrawing of a bolt and the rattle of a chain. The door opened wide enough to allow an old woman's face to peer out at me, suspicion speckling her eyes. I identified myself and showed the fruit to reassure her. Then there was another pause before the door gradually opened to reveal an old woman leaning heavily on a walking stick. Inviting me in, she hobbled off slowly and painfully down the hall and into her tiny living room. She made me sit down and, despite my polite protests, proceeded to make me a cup of tea. The room resembled a kind of grotto, adorned with religious objects and pictures. Her rosary beads hung from the fireplace clock and a black cat slept on the rug-covered sofa. She talked to me from the kitchen as she worked.

'Isn't the weather terrible?'

'Desperate – you'd never think it was the summer,' I replied, smiling as I listened to myself. I had started to sound like Gerry Breen's apprentice.

'Summers never used to be like this. I can remember summers when the streets were baked hot as an oven and everyone used to sit on their doorsteps for you could hardly get a breath. If you sat on your doorstep these past few days you'd get pneumonia.'

She brought me a cup of tea in a china cup, and a slice of fruit cake, but nothing for herself. She sat down and scrutinised me intently.

'So you're working for Gerry for the summer. I'm sure that's good fun for you. You work hard and maybe he'll keep you on permanent.'

I didn't correct her misunderstanding, but I laughed silently inside.

'He says if it keeps on raining he's going to start building an ark.'

She smiled and rearranged the cushion supporting her back.

'Gerry's the salt of the earth. Do you see that fruit you

187

brought? He's been doing that for the best part of fifteen years and nobody knows but him and me.'

She paused to pour more tea into my cup and I listened with curiosity as she continued, her words making me feel as if I was looking at a familiar object from a new and unexpected perspective.

'I gave him a wee bit of help a long time ago and he's never forgotten it, not through all these years. I don't get out much now, but sometimes I take a walk round to the shop, just to see how he's getting on. He's a great man for the crack, isn't he?'

I smiled in agreement and she shuffled forward in her seat, leaning confidentially towards me.

'Have you met Lady Muck yet? Thon woman's more airs and graces than royalty. She was born and bred a stone's throw from here and to listen to her now you'd think she came from the Malone Road. I knew her family and they didn't have two pennies to rub together between the lot of them. Now she traipses round the town like she was a duchess. You'll never catch her serving behind the counter.'

It was obvious that the woman wanted to talk – she was probably starved of company – and no matter how often I attempted a polite exit, she insisted on my staying a little longer, assuring me that Gerry wouldn't mind. I wasn't so sure, but there was no easy escape, as she produced a photograph album and talked me through a maze of memories and mementoes.

Parts of it were interesting and when she told me about the Belfast blitz I learned things I hadn't known before. Before I finally got up to go, she returned to the subject of the weather, her voice serious and solemn.

'This weather's a sign. I've been reading about it in a tract that was sent to me. It's by this holy scholar, very high up in the church, and he says we're living in the last days. All these wars and famines – they're all signs. All this rain – it's a sign too. I believe it.'

When she opened the front door it was still raining and I almost started to believe it too. I ran back quickly, partly to get out of the rain and partly because I anticipated a rebuke about the length of my absence.

There were no customers in the shop when I entered and he merely lifted his head from what he was reading, asked if everything was all right with Mrs McCausland, and returned to his study. It surprised me a little that he said nothing about the time. He was filling in his pools coupon and concentrating on winning a fortune, so perhaps he was distracted by the complexities of the Australian leagues. He had been doing them all summer and his approach never varied. He did two columns every week, the first by studying the form and this forced him to ponder such probabilities as whether Inala City would draw with Slacks Creek, or Altona with Bulleen. For the second column, he selected random numbers, his eyes screwed up and an expression on his face as if he was waiting for some kind of celestial message. On this particular afternoon, reception must have been bad, because he asked me to shout them out. Out of genuine curiosity, I asked him what he would do if he did win a fortune. He looked at me to see if I was winding him up, but must have sensed that I wasn't, because, on a wet and miserable Belfast afternoon, he told me his dream.

'It's all worked out in here,' he said, tapping the side of his head with a chisel-shaped finger. 'I've it all planned out. Thinking about it keeps you going – makes you feel better on days like this.'

He paused to check if I was laughing at him, then took a hand out of his coat pocket and gestured slowly round the shop.

'Look around you, son. What do you see?'

A still, grey light seemed to have filtered into the shop. The lights were off and it was quiet in an almost eerie way. Nothing rustled or stirred, and the only sound was the soft fall of the rain. In the gloom the bright colours smouldered like embers; rhubarb like long tongues of flame; red sparks of apples; peaches, perfect in their velvety softness, yellows and oranges flickering gently.

'Fruit,' I answered. 'Different kinds of fruit.'

'Now, do you know what I see?'

I shook my head.

'I see places. A hundred different places. Look again.' And as he spoke he began to point with his finger. 'Oranges from Spain, apples from New Zealand, cabbages from Holland, peaches from Italy, grapes from the Cape, bananas from Ecuador – fruit from all over the world. Crops grown and harvested by hands I never see, packed and transported by other hands in a chain that brings them here to me. It's a miracle if you think about it. When we're sleeping in our beds, hands all over the world are picking and packing so that Gerry Breen can sell it here in this shop.'

We both stood and looked, absorbing the magnitude of the miracle.

'You asked me what I'd do if I won the jackpot – well, I've it all thought out. I'd go to every country whose fruit I sell, go and see it grow, right there in the fields and the groves, in the orchards and the vineyards. All over the world.'

He looked at me out of the corner of his eye to see if I thought he was crazy, then turned away and began to tidy the counter. I didn't say anything, but in that moment, if he'd asked me, I would have gone with him. All these years later, I still regret that I didn't tell him that. Told him while there was still time.

Four days later, Gerry Breen was dead. A man walked into the shop and shot him twice. He became another bystander, another nobody, sucked into the vortex by a random and malignant fate that marked him out. They needed a Catholic to balance the score – he became a casualty of convenience, a victim of retribution, propitiation of a different god. No one even claimed it. Just one more sectarian murder – unclaimed, unsolved, soon unremembered but by a few. A name lost in the anonymity of a long list. I would forget too, but I can't.

I remember it all. There were no customers when a motorbike stopped outside with two men on it. The engine was still running as the passenger came towards the shop. I was behind the counter looking out. He had one hand inside his black motorcycle tunic and wore a blue crash helmet – the type that encloses the whole head. A green scarf covered the bottom half of his face, so only his eyes were visible. Only his eyes – that's all I ever saw of him. Mr

Breen was standing holding a tray of oranges he had just brought from the back.

Suddenly, the man pulled a gun out of his tunic and I thought we were going to be robbed, but he never spoke, and as he raised the gun and pointed at Mr Breen, his hand was shaking so much he had to support it with the other one. It was then I knew he hadn't come for money. The first shot hit Gerry Breen in the chest, spinning him round, and as he slumped to the floor the oranges scattered and rolled in all directions. He lay there, face down, and his body was still moving. Then, as I screamed an appeal for mercy, the man walked forward and, kneeling over the body, shot him in the back of the head. His body kicked and shuddered, and then was suddenly and unnaturally still. I screamed again in fear and anger and then, pointing the gun at me, the man walked slowly backwards to the door of the shop, ran to the waiting bike and was gone. Shaking uncontrollably and stomach heaving with vomit, I tried to turn Mr Breen over on to his back, but he was too heavy for me. Blood splashed his green coat, and flowed from the dark gaping wound, streaming across the floor, mixing with the oranges that were strewn all around us. Oranges from Spain.

They say help arrived almost immediately. I don't know. All I can remember is thinking of the old woman's words and hoping it really was the end of the world, and being glad and asking God to drown the world, wanting it to rain for a thousand years, rain and rain and never stop until all the blood was washed away and every street was washed clean. There were voices then and helping hands trying to lift me away, but no one could move me as I knelt beside him, clutching frantically at his green coat, begging God not to let him die, praying he'd let Gerry Breen live to build his ark and bring aboard the fruit of the world. All the fruit of the world safely stored. Oranges from Spain, apples from the Cape – the sweet taste of summer preserved for ever, eternal and in-corruptible.